MIDLIFE MAGIC MIRROR

LEGACY WITCHES OF SHADOW COVE

JENNIFER L. HART

D1526042

ELEMENTS UNLEASHED

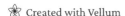

MIDLIFE MAGIC MIRROR

Midlife Magic Mirror
Hart/ Jennifer L.

1.Women's—Fiction 2. North Carolina—Fiction 3.
Paranormal—Fiction 4. Witch Romance—Fiction 5.
Demons Romance—Fiction 6.Twins—Fiction 7. Small
Towns—Fiction 8. Decluttering—Fiction 9. American
Humorous—Fiction 10.Mountain Living —Fiction 11.
Divorce— Fiction 12. Shifter Romance—Fiction I. Title

ISBN: 9798397880800

One fortysomething mama with an empty nest. One middle-aged witch who fights wraiths. For each of the Sanders sisters, looking at her twin is like gazing at her reflection in a funhouse mirror—warped, twisted, and a little bit scary.

Donna Sanders has done everything right. She has created a successful home-organizing business and distanced herself from her crazy twin—the witch of Shadow Cove. Donna is completely blindsided when her husband locks her out of the house and demands a divorce.

With nowhere else to turn, Donna moves back to her childhood home, a creepy gothic house on the outskirts of town. The cauldron of bats in the attic she can handle. The ghost of the passive-aggressive Southern debutant doesn't faze her. But living with her sister and her endless parade of witchy secrets is a fate worse than death.

Donna's only reprieve is flirting with Axel, her sister's handsome and much too young for her personal assistant. But even the sexy younger man is more than what he seems. Can this late-blooming witch learn to embrace her gifts and find love before Bella's dark past catches up with them both?

Midlife Magic Mirror is book 1 of the Legacy Witches of Shadow Cove series. If you like supernatural tales about magical destinies, midlife shifts, and bonds of sisterhood, you don't want to miss *USA Today* bestselling author Jennifer L. Hart's bewitching book. Buy *Midlife Magic Mirror* and invoke your inner power today!

This one is for Traci/Gentry Lee/Liane/Nyx/mama diva/the mermaid.

Whatever name you go by you are beautiful inside and out.

CONTENT WARNING

This book contains witchcraft, violence, themes of rape and abuse, as well as characters overcoming past trauma. I try to handle these themes with love and respect but if they are too much for you as a reader, you might want to skip this book.

Love and light,
Jennifer L. Hart

MIDLIFE MAGIC MIRROR

CHAPTER 1
DONNA

Some days I had the adulting thing down. Then there were days I spit toothpaste in my own hair.

"What the shit?"

Shifting my binder, phone, shoulder bag, and umbrella to my left side, I fumbled with the keys, wondering if I had used the wrong one. Why else wouldn't it fit in the lock? I'd color-coded each bow with different nail polish to keep exactly that from happening. Mysterious Purple for the garage, Crimson Skies for the office I never used for anything but storage, and Golden Sands for the storage locker that held my surplus projects. It had been a very long day and my mind was back at the college campus where I'd just left my son for the start of his freshman fall semester.

I squinted at the key, already on the verge of panic. I lost things. Important things. More often than I wanted to admit. Nope, that was the key with Seafoam painted on the flat. The binder with all the fabric samples fell out of my hand and landed face-down in a puddle as I attempted to reinsert the key. Frustration made tears mingle with the rain.

Okay, self, deep breath. Focus. All I wanted was to get out of these wet clothes, pour a glass of wine, and sit in my oversized bathtub until I thawed out. Why, today of all days, did everything have to be so frigging difficult?

"Because you have ADHD," I muttered the answer to my own question. "Because your frigging brain makes everything more frigging difficult, Donna."

The brain I'd had for forty-four years was neurodivergent. The diagnosis was relatively new. I hadn't been a disruptive child who bounced off the walls during class. I didn't make scenes and didn't disrupt the other students. Even if my mother would have listened to conventional advice, there had been no need to go to a doctor or try out a prescription. No, I just quietly read what I wanted to read instead of the things I was supposed to be reading. I quietly developed my ways to cope with hyperfocus, tuning out, and time blindness. I quietly slipped through the cracks.

In its own way, my wonky brain had done me a solid. It forced me to develop coping strategies to function. My key method hadn't failed me before so clearly, something else was amiss.

Warm rain beat down on my umbrella and ran in rivulets around me as I crouched down to study the doorknob. The brass doorknob. I stared at it for a long moment, trying to reconcile what I was seeing. The knob was new. As in brand-spanking new. No gouges or scratches from fumbling with keys. It was also ugly and didn't quite cover the unpainted section the previous oil-rubbed bronze had because it had been oval, not circular.

"What the hell is going on here?" Could there have been some sort of accident? A tree fell through the front door, smashing the old handle and lock set. Yeah, I could picture that. If so, why hadn't Lewis called me to let me know what had happened?

After shifting a load of stuff to one hand, I tried my husband's cell. Straight to voicemail. He'd left the campus early, stating he had things to do for work. I had wanted to lean on him on the day that had tied my insides into anxious knots, sending my lone chick out to fly from the nest. But Lewis wasn't the strong supportive type of husband. Most of the time I had to work around him. Better for everyone that he'd left.

A gust of wind almost ripped my umbrella from my hands. Ridiculous. I could just go in through the garage door. The mystery of the changed lock could wait until I had a big glass of sweet red coursing through my system. Glaring at the shitty door knob one last time, I slogged my way down the concrete steps and over the garden path to the garage door. All the fine hairs stood up on my neck when I saw the twin to the front door lock with an accompanying deadbolt barring my way.

I tried Lewis again. When his voicemail picked up right away, I left a terse message. "It's Donna. I'm locked out of the house. Call me as soon as you get this."

Thunder rumbled overhead and I shivered. Water had soaked through my sneakers and my socks were soggy. No one was out on our street so at least no one was witnessing my humiliation. Then again, it would be nice if one of my neighbors invited me out of the storm to wait.

I could sit in my car. The little silver Impala had heat. Or I could drive into town, maybe go to the coffee shop and wait for Lewis to turn on his damn phone. But my wine and bathtub were on the other side of those accursed locks. This was my home, damn it. My refuge from the world. Something I badly needed.

If I'd been younger, less stressed, or had less of a wonky brain, I might have made another decision. But I was cold and wet and sad and just done.

Fuck it, I would break into my own house.

The patio door that overlooked the backyard was a slider. The natural choice. It would be a pain in the ass to replace. But I'd spring for the double French doors I'd always wanted and Lewis would just have to suck up the cost.

Clutching my umbrella in one hand, I went to the paver walkway I'd started putting in a few months ago and hadn't gotten around to finishing. The bricks were stacked in a heap and I snagged one off the top, knocking several others into a mud puddle. Because of the work that I did moving boxes and bins and furniture, I was stronger than I looked for a plus-sized middle-aged mom. A healthy shot of annoyance helped to fuel my throw. The brick sailed through the air like a missile and hit the sliding glass door dead center. Glass exploded inwards, pebbling the way it was supposed to do for the sake of safety instead of breaking into massive shards.

The alarm started blaring.

Pleased with the result, I hurried forward to shut it

off. Once I punched in the code that let our security company know that all was well, I'd cover the hole. There should still be some plywood in the garage. I would just get it and drill it into the door frame....

My thoughts stopped dead in their tracks when I spotted them. Lewis, pants around his ankles, was staring at me. As was the whip cream-covered tart who had her bare ass perched on my granite countertops.

We all just looked at each other for a long moment.

"Are you crazy?" Lewis's thick dark eyebrows drew together as he broke the silence.

"My key didn't work." It was a stupid thing to say. To shout actually since the alarm was still going off.

The woman smirked at me. "And you didn't take the hint?"

The sound of her voice, so familiar even though I had never met her in person, burst the surreal bubble. "So, this is what was so important, Lewis? This is what you had to do instead of spending the day with your *son*. You had to bang your frigging secretary in my frigging kitchen? What's the rush, Lewis? The Viagra gonna wear off?"

Lewis flushed to his receding hairline and struggled to fasten his trousers even as he jabbed a finger at me. "It's over, Donna. You might as well just leave."

"Leave?" I stared at him blankly. "Why should I leave? This is my house. I decorated it. I picked out every stick of furniture and painting in every room. I hand-selected every rug and curtain and unlike some people, I make sure mine always match." This last was directed at the bottle blonde with a pointed look at her crotch.

She huffed and crossed her arms, opened her mouth to retort. I wasn't interested in anything Mindy had to say. Especially when someone started pounding on the front door.

"Shit," Lewis muttered and then headed for the hallway, tucking in his shirt as he went. The whip cream-covered tart reached for a purple halter dress and slid it on. I stood there, dripping on the pebbled glass, glaring daggers at her and feeling....

Old. Tired. But not even a little bit surprised. I'd seen the signs for months. The late nights at the office, the sudden business trips. The not-so-subtle ways he'd shut the door to his home office to make phone calls. Maybe other men were better at hiding their affairs, but not Lewis. Or maybe it was my wonky brain making me more aware of his emotions. In retrospect, I wondered if he'd wanted to be caught. Deep down we both knew he was a coward. He avoided conflict. Hell, the passive-aggressive little stain had changed the locks to my freaking house instead of admitting he didn't want to be married any longer. I was the hothead, the ballbuster. The one with the temper who threw bricks.

There was a steady sound of beeping and then finally, the alarm shut off. My pulse pounded in my ears.

"That's her," Lewis said.

Glancing up I saw that he was pointing his stubby index finger at me. "She's the one who broke in."

My jaw dropped. "This is my house!"

The cops, two young men who didn't appear much older than my son, exchanged a look. One picked up the brick. "Did you break this door, ma'am?"

Ma'am. Insult to injury. "Yes, but—"

"You're coming with us," the taller of the two said as his partner moved behind me.

"You have the right to remain silent."

I was being read my rights. Handcuffs closed shut around my wrists. Holy hell, this was actually happening.

"Lewis," I begged. "Tell them who I am!"

He folded his arms over his chest and said nothing. The smug little toad.

The rain had stopped by the time I was perp-marched out of my beloved home. All my neighbors were by their windows, watching as I was loaded into the back of a squad car and taken downtown.

I COULDN'T HOLD A THOUGHT. Not when I was fingerprinted or when the admitting officer took my photo. Not when my purse was searched or when I was told to strip down out of my wet jeans, sneakers, and t-shirt and given a stiff polyester jumpsuit to change into.

"You get a phone call." The bored-sounding female police officer—who had given me more action with a pat down than Lewis had in the last few years—informed me.

A phone call. Okay, that was good. Except, whom should I call? Bad enough that gossip would be spreading around our small mountain town that Lewis Allen had his crazy wife arrested. Who would not only bail my wrongfully detained hide from the clink but would help me find a place to stay?

There was only one name that came to mind. One person I knew who would show up in my hour of need. I really, *really* didn't want to make that call. We hadn't seen each other in almost a year.

In the end, I didn't have a choice.

"Yo," a male voice answered the phone.

I rolled my eyes. "Is Bella there?"

"Who?"

I huffed out a breath. "Bella Sanders. This is her phone."

"No way," the guy said. "The Bella Sanders? The witch of Shadow Cove?"

"Just an ugly rumor," I heard someone say.

"Snap." The guy who was holding Bella's phone and —thereby me—hostage said.

I gritted out. "May I speak to her, please?"

On the other end of the line there was the rustling of what I assumed were sheets. Where else would my sister keep Mr. Insightful but chained to her bed?

"Um, like, who's calling?" he asked. I couldn't place his accent. Southern, but not North Carolina. Maybe Texas?

Where did she find this mensa candidate? "Tell her it's Donna."

"Yo, hot stuff, you wanna talk to a Don?" The phone guy must be high.

"Don*na*," I snarled.

"I've got it," a familiar female voice murmured. "Hello?"

"It's me." The desk sergeant was giving me an impatient look. I had a bad feeling that he would announce time was up at any moment and march down the hall to take me to my cell.

"Well hello, sis. Nice of you to call." Bella sounded the same way she always did. Slightly amused, and as though she harbored a mischievous secret.

I closed my eyes and forced the words out. "Listen, I need you to come down to the jail and bail me out."

"Jail?" I could hear the smugness in her voice. "Virtuous little Donna in jail? What are you in for? Ripping tags off the mattresses?"

My teeth ground together. "It's a long story."

"I've got time," Bella purred.

"Time's up," the desk sergeant announced.

My knuckles turned white where they gripped the phone. "Bella, please. I have never asked you for anything since—" I cut myself off, not wanting to admit anything incriminating where we would be overheard. "Please I... need you."

Silence on the other end. "Fine, I'll be there when I can."

"Thank you," I breathed right before the desk sergeant snatched the phone out of my hands and hung it up.

I was the only person currently in lockup. My knee bounced up and down in my scratchy jumpsuit as I waited. The confrontation wouldn't be pretty. It was definitely a toothpaste-in-the-hair kinda day.

I sensed Bella's arrival before I saw her. It was a twin thing. Sharing our mother's womb for eight and a half months forged a connection between us. One that's damn near impossible to break.

Even though we were identical twins, Bella and I were night and day. I kept my black hair cut to my shoulders and had the white strands colored to hide my real age. As far as I knew, Bella's never had a haircut. Her hair was so long she could sit on the mermaid tresses. The salt and pepper look had her aging gracefully and beautifully whereas I looked haggard and unkempt when my roots began to show.

Though we possessed the same small upturned nose, the same vivid green eyes, the same pale skin, and puffy pink lips, Bella's features combined into a more sensual package. It's something about the way she presented herself and commanded attention whenever she entered a room.

Or maybe it was her magic.

Ten seconds after my twin tingle activated, I saw the desk sergeant try to suck in his gut. Then I heard her voice, husky and melodic. "Is my sister here?"

"Yes, Ms. Sanders." His gaze flitted down and I turned away so I didn't have to see him drooling over her.

Some things never changed. Even with my wonky brain, I was the forgettable sister. The one who guys thought of as a buddy who could put in a good word with my sister when we were both in school. The one called on to run the homeowner's association because I would not only take the thankless job seriously, I would make sure to bring nut-free, gluten-free, dairy-free treats for the Fourth of July block party because I'd had a last-minute impulsive need to up the ante. Better to overcompensate and put up a good front so no one knew I was defective. I may have been forty-five minutes late, but damn it, I came through in a big way.

Whereas Bella...well, no one had ever invited my sister to take charge of anything. Partly because she was an exotic butterfly that no one wanted to burden with pesky details. And partly because they believed the rumors about our family.

"Well well, how the mighty have fallen," Bella murmured from behind me.

"What's that supposed to...?" I trailed off as my gaze fell to her belly.

My sister was heavily pregnant.

CHAPTER 2
BELLA

I could say it didn't fill me with a grim sort of satisfaction to see high and mighty Donna Sanders-Allen speechless for once in our lives. Or that it didn't tickle me because even though she had claimed to have no place for me and my witchy weirdness in her life that I was the person she'd called when the chips were down. I could say all that.

But I'd be lying.

She looked like hell. Not just because she was wearing prison-issue polyester and her hair had frizzed as it air-dried. No, it was more something in her aura that made her look so sick...so broken as she stared at my baby bump. Then the barrage of questions started.

"How?"

"Do I need to draw you a diagram?" I raised an eyebrow. "Or I could make the hand gesture."

She shook her head. "Who...? Where...? What...?"

"Colonel Mustard in the Conservatory with the Lead Pipe," I waggled my eyebrows at her.

"Huh?" She shook her head. "You never make any sense."

I studied my chipping black sparkle nail polish. "You could just say 'Congratulations, Bella. I'm so happy for you,' and call it a day."

Her stony green gaze met mine. "Congratulations."

It sounded like a curse. My lips curled up in an involuntary smile. Oh, this was delicious. "And maybe tag on a thank you for coming to bail my cranky carcass out of lock-up? How much is your bail, by the way?"

"I'll pay you back."

She would but not with money. I kept that tidbit to myself because I didn't want her to change her mind. Donna was prickly at the best of times and going by the sorry state of her aura, today hadn't been the best of times.

I snapped my finger, putting a little extra intention behind the gesture. The officer who had been staring at my ass a moment earlier hopped forward.

I turned to face the grizzled man, looked him square in the eyes, and pushed my power into his mind. Ephemeral tendrils snaked out from me into him like wisps of smoke, binding him to me. Reflections on a human brain were a simple matter. In my eyes, which had turned to mirrors, the other party saw what they wanted to see, instead of what was truly there.

And this chubby, passed-over middle-aged dude whose wife had left him for her dance instructor wanted to be someone's hero.

Behind me, Donna made an exasperated sound. "Really, Bells?"

JENNIFER L. HART

"Do you want to wait around for a bail hearing?" I asked her without breaking my stare.

Sure, the peek I took into people's minds was an invasion of privacy. But I'd been given my gift for a reason. Why bog myself down the way Donna did with moral issues of right vs. wrong?

Besides, most people were incredibly boring.

"I need your help." Adopting the role that would help the spell along, I leaned forward and clutched the officer's arm. "There's been a terrible mistake."

Donna snorted. I ignored her as I played up my damsel in distress act. "My sister is desperately ill and needs to get to the doctor right away. You're the only one who can help us!"

He shook his head. The fog of my influence hung around him like a cloud, blocking out training and rules and procedures that he was supposed to follow. "Well, I ...uh...."

"Please." I beseeched him with my mirrored eyes. "Please be our hero."

That did it. He glanced around and then strode forward with purpose, keys in hand. I sent Donna a smug smile as the lock clicked and the door swung open. Though she didn't appreciate my using magic on the common folk, I sensed her relief. Our kind didn't do well locked in a cage.

Even if it was one of our own making. Like my twin's.

Donna collected her soggy belongings. I told the sergeant to erase all evidence that Donna had ever been there, and then we headed outside. Donna hunched her shoulders as if that would prevent downtown Shadow

14

Cove from seeing us together. Puddles lined the street but the Carolina sun was peeking out from behind the clouds. The sunset that evening would be utterly glorious.

I made my way over to my jade-green coup DeVille convertible and inserted the key. The car was vintage 1970 and had cost me a pretty penny in restoring. Well worth it though as it was my favorite accessory.

"Top up or down?" I asked Donna as I fished my rhinestone sunglasses out of my beaded purse.

She sent me a panicked look. "Up!"

"Killjoy," I quipped but left the top in place even though I longed to feel the wind in my hair.

Donna scrambled into the seat and then hunched down low.

"Seatbelt," I chirped.

Oh, if looks could kill I'd be a stain on the upholstery.

"It's the law." Teasing her was too much fun.

She wriggled around, doing her best to stay hidden from view and fasten her seatbelt at the same time.

I turned the key in the ignition and relished the growl of the engine. "There are spare shades and a scarf in the glove box," I murmured as I backed out of the slanted space.

She dove for the compartment. Withdrew the Hermès scarf and wrapped it around her head before slipping the oversized round shades into place. "You're having way too much fun at my expense. And you're going the wrong way."

Shit. "Just enough for both of us, like always." I made an illegal U-turn and headed toward her house in the little cookie-cutter subdivision that was straight out of a sitcom from the 1980s. "So, are you going to tell me why you were in jail?"

She crossed her arms over her ample chest. "Like the way you told me you were pregnant?"

"You ordered me to stay out of your life, Donna. I was trying to respect your wishes." Foolish though they might be.

I heard her inhale and then swallow. "Lewis changed the locks on me."

My head whipped around. "He did *what*?"

"Look out!" Donna shrieked as the front tire on the passenger's side went up on the sidewalk.

I swore and then course corrected. "You've got to be shitting me. You've castrated yourself to be the perfect little Suzie homemaker. And that ungrateful bastard locked you out? That's it, I'm turning him into a fungus."

"You'll do no such thing." Donna's voice took on that prim lecturing tone. "The last thing we need is you reviving all the talk about magic again. Especially right before you give birth."

I didn't respond, still trying to get my head around what she'd told me. "Did you two have a fight or something?"

She shook her head. "No. You know Lewis isn't big on confrontation. He just started screwing his secretary and —" Her sentence cut off in a scream as I slammed on the brakes.

"He's been *cheating* on you?" At that moment I wouldn't have been surprised if smoke started billowing from my nostrils.

Donna looked out at the mountain laurels that lined the road. "Yeah."

I felt the life inside me move and shift. Clearly, my offspring shared my outrage. "So let me get this straight. Lewis the future fungus was cheating on you and locked you out of your own home. And you expect me to do *nothing*?"

The last word was practically a shriek.

Donna put a hand on her scarf-covered head. "You've already done enough by getting me out of there."

"You are not going back to him," I snarled.

"That's for me to decide," she growled back.

"In case you've forgotten, you're a Sanders," I hissed. "A legacy witch from a proud and distinguished line. We protect Shadow Cove. The mundane assholes in this town do *not* get to screw us over."

Donna

AND THERE SHE went with the legacy witch crap. The same hoopla that my mother and grandmother had been filling our heads with since we were knee-high to grasshoppers.

"Are you forgetting that I'm the dud?" I whispered. "No magic, so no special witch benefits."

"You are not a dud," Bella snapped. "You chose to live a boring-ass mundane life. To pretend that you didn't have any gifts. But that doesn't mean people can treat you like dirt."

17

. . .

"I can't get into this right now." My head was pounding. I desperately wanted to lie down in a dark room and sleep for a week, not diffuse the Bella bomb. "Can I just... stay with you for a while?"

I couldn't see her eyes behind her tinted sunglasses but could feel her gaze. "You want to stay with me?"

Want had nothing to do with it. "If that's all right?"

Another long moment passed and for an instant, I was afraid she would refuse me. My brain started churning out backup plans. I could go to a hotel. Or maybe find a short-term rental. But the truth was that neither of those options appealed to me. As outrageous as Bella was, at least I knew she was in my corner. She'd come to my rescue and while I might not approve of her methods, I couldn't argue with the results.

"Please," I whispered.

She nodded once and cut the wheel hard. The DeVille curb checked again as my sister made another illegal U-turn. Then we were heading away from town and climbing up the steep hillside that led to the knob over-looking the mundane community of Shadow Cove.

It was a solid ten minutes of taking switchbacks up the hillside. Ten minutes for me to steal surreptitious glances at her baby bump and wonder about it. Was this planned? Who was the father? That guy who answered Bella's phone? I hoped not. Thinking about his burn-out DNA mingling in our gene pool gave me shivers.

The gothic mansion emerged before us like a nightmare vision created by a twisted mind. Which it was. According to family lore our three times great grandmother Edith Sanders had convinced her wealthy husband-to-be to build Storm Grove for her as a wedding present. The husband hadn't survived the honeymoon though. A boating accident on Shadow Lake was what the papers had reported. A great whirlpool had opened and swallowed up his entire vessel. One of those freak things.

Edith had moved into the manor by herself and had delivered her twin daughters, Jasmine, and Esmerelda.

Twin girls had been the norm for Sanders women ever since. Twin girls who'd grown up on the property. Who, like salmon, came home once more when it was time to spawn. Up until I'd broken the chain by getting married and having Devon.

"How far along are you?" I asked Bella as we passed by the ten-foot-tall iron gates that lead to Storm Grove Manor.

"Seven months," she murmured.

"Twins I assume?" It was Bella. She would uphold the family tradition even if she had to drink a chromosome cocktail to do it.

She shrugged and then parked the DeVille adjacent to the front door. "Only time will tell."

"You're going to need a different car."

She lowered her sunglasses down her nose and just stared at me.

"It's a two-door," I pointed out. "Car seats take up a lot of room."

"So, I should give up everything I love and buy a

minivan? Hide from my gifts and take up bake sales and the PTA? Become part of a community of the uninspired and insipid?" Bella raised a brow. "How's that working out for you, sis?"

Ouch.

Bella got out of the car and slammed the door. Since the driver's side window was still down she leaned back down and stared at me.

"In case you've forgotten, Donna, we were born for more important things than playing nice with the mundane people of Shadow Cove. Like keeping them safe."

"Safe from what?" I threw my hands up in the air. "Bella, it's all make-believe. There are no wraiths! There is no portal to protect. It's all fantasy. Mom wasn't abducted by demons, she abandoned us!"

"Believe what you want. You always do anyway," she murmured.

I watched as she sashayed up the stairs with the peeling paint, past the two gargoyles that I'd named Clyde and Hyde, and into the house. We'd been having a variation on the same exact argument for two and a half decades. Bella, like our mother, Fiona, and our grand-mother Ruth—aka Grand—believed that there were invisible evil spirits that crept into people's dreams, took over their bodies, and made them do tasks that would open portals to hell. That these wraiths answered to demons who were determined to take over the world. And that our family was tasked with guarding the portal and stopping them.

It had been a fun fantasy when I was in elementary

school. What little girl didn't want to believe that she would one day hold an important job, one that would protect everyone and everything she loved from evil? But after years without any sign of magic, I'd forced myself to face the truth. My family had abilities. But they didn't mean anything. There was no great destiny. No good reason why we couldn't lead normal lives instead of holing up at this decaying property forever apart from the world. Mom and Grand were batshit crazy. I'd tried to reason with Bella more times than I could count. Tried to convince her she could have something other than the Sander's legacy. But she hadn't listened. And when mom had left when we'd been seniors in high school, it had been up to me to break the cycle.

Yeah, so maybe life with Lewis hadn't been exciting or mysterious. The big reason I'd married him was *because* he was so predictable. I'd needed that after years of living in chaos. Devon had thrived on the routine. I'd sent him off to college on a soccer scholarship. I'd done better for my son than our mother had done for us. Up to and including keeping my distance from my delusional twin and shutting down the rumors about the Sanders women being bugfuck crazy.

And where had that gotten me? Right back to where I'd started. Damn Lewis and the makers of ED medication right to the bowels of hell. How come scientists could cure limp dicks but we still had nothing to combat middle-aged weight gain, fatigue, or hot flashes? We were told to better control our diet and exercise more because goddess knows that fistful of raisins I'd scarfed mid-day while helping my son set up his dorm room was the height of indulgence. Clyde and Hyde stared at me, their hideous scrunched-up faces mocking me. Panic flared. I didn't want to go into that house. Just being near it made me twitchy. I dug my phone out of my purse and dialed Lewis's number.

"Donna?" he answered on the third ring.

I shut my eyes and took a deep breath. I would not yell or scream or belittle him in any way. I'd always managed to smooth over the rough patches before. There was too much at stake. Of course, I had never walked in on him having sex with someone else before either. But still, we had been together for twenty-two years. We had a son. We had made a good team. Surely we could find some common ground.

Goals set, I began in an even voice. "Lewis, listen to me. This has all gotten so out of control and I think we need to sit down and—"

"I want a divorce," he blurted out.

"What?" I must have misheard.

"I've already filed the paperwork," he continued. "You'll get the documents next week."

I shook my head. "This doesn't make any sense."

But he'd already hung up.

CHAPTER 3
DONNA

My gaze was fixed on the external buttresses, the pointed arches, and the asymmetrical design of Storm Grove Manor. It sat forbidding and starkly shadowed against the final rays of the dying August sun. I didn't see any of them though as I stared off into the ether.

This wasn't the plan.

Someone knocked on the passenger's side window. I jumped. The guy standing there looked like he'd gotten lost on his way to the beach. Shaggy blond hair, deep tan, whiter-than-the-driven-snow-smile. He wore cargo shorts and an unbuttoned Hawaiian shirt with sandals on his feet. I'd seen dozens like him at the campus earlier. Dollars to doughnuts he was the guy who'd picked up Bella's phone. I'd die of shock if he was a day over twenty-five.

Beach bum dude made a motion for me to roll down the window and after a moment's hesitation, I did.

"You okay?" He had pretty gray eyes, like an early morning fog that wrapped around a body and kissed it with mist.

I recognized the Texas accent right away. Sure enough, this was the dim bulb who'd picked up Bella's phone when I'd called. Young, dumb, and unless I missed my guess, hung. My sister sure could pick 'em.

At least he was kind for checking up on me. "Yeah, I'm fine. Who are you?"

"I'm Axel." He stuck his hand through the window. "You must be Don."

"Donna," I corrected but took the proffered hand. It was warm and rough, lightly calloused. Touching him sent an electric current zinging through my system. It was on the tip of my tongue to ask if he was Bella's baby daddy but decided against it. "What are you doing here, Axel?"

"Didn't Bells tell you? I'm her new assistant."

"So that's what the kids are calling it these days," I grumbled.

"What?" Axel's heavy blond brows pulled together, though he kept smiling. He was cute. Like a modern-day Viking who'd taken one too many hits to the noggin.

"Never mind." If my twin wanted to move her barely legal baby daddy into the family home, who the hell was I to judge?

"You coming in anytime soon?" Axel asked me. "It's almost cocktail hour. I'm making mojitos."

"My sister's pregnant. She shouldn't be drinking," I lectured.

He flashed me a grin. "That's why I make all of hers virgin."

It was on the tip of my tongue to snark that she might have developed a taste for virgins but held back. It wasn't Axel's fault that I was having the shittiest day of my life. He didn't deserve my snark. "A mojito sounds amazing."

"No bags?" Axel asked as he held the car door open for me.

I shook my head. I had nothing on me other than what had been on my person. Being out in the world without my stuff left me feeling naked. Vulnerable.

Axel slung an arm around my shoulders. "No worries, Don. I'm sure Bells has some stuff you can borrow."

I shuddered at the thought. My sister liked to dress like a goth version of Stevie Nicks. Not exactly my style.

"Come on, let's get you a drink."

As he led me up the stone steps past Hyde and Clyde, I had to grudgingly admit that I liked this kid. Even if he couldn't be bothered to say my full name.

The foyer was as large and intimidating as ever. The vertical proportions stretched to the ceiling three stories above. Skinny spindled railings clung to the curved staircase that led to the upper levels. Black and what wasn't black, was stone. The space was cold and foreboding, with no furniture or drop zones or anything that was remotely welcoming or useful. It was like a stop on a ghost tour more than a home.

With no fabrics to soften the sound, our footsteps echoed in the space as we crossed into the main drawing room. The stone fireplace was large enough to stand in and dominated one wall between two stained glass windows that came to points in the center. A burgundy chaise longue faced the fireplace and an old-fashioned dry bar cart sat alongside it. Axel guided me to the chaise before turning his attention to the cart. I watched as he mixed the rum, and lime juice and then muddled what smelled like basil.

"No mint?" I asked when he handed me the drink.

He flashed a dimple at me. "Just try it."

I did. It had a fresh taste like a classic Mojito but was a little spicier. "Wow, that's really good."

"I used to work as a mixologist. We had a bumper crop of basil this year and I just finished harvesting it from the garden. Hope you like pesto."

"It's one of my favorites," I admitted.

"Marvelous," he grinned and went back to mixing.

Bella swept into the room, her white eyelet broom-stick skirt swishing around her ankles. She gave Axel a peck on the cheek as he handed her the next drink. "Be a love and get the green room ready for my sister."

"No, I can—" I made to set my drink aside, but Axel waved at me, indicating I should stay where I was.

"It's no trouble, Don." He winked at me and then sauntered from the room.

Bella tilted her head to watch his ass as he ascended the stairs.

"He's barely older than Devon," I said to her. "Have you no shame?"

"None," Bella said and then turned her full focus on me. "Besides, he's a great help to me here."

"Since when do you need an assistant?" I raised a brow at her. "It's not like you work for a living."

"Just because I don't have a traditional nine-to-five slog doesn't mean I don't earn my keep," Bella said. "And the wraith attacks have been increasing the past several months. Not a night goes by that I don't have to free some poor soul from being hijacked."

Not again. I finished my drink and got up to fix myself another. I was going to need it. "Bella, there are perfectly logical explanations why people do things that are seemingly out of character."

"Yes, they are called wraiths." She huffed out a sigh as though I were the one being difficult.

"No, they are called drugs, alcohol, depression, mood disorders, mixing medications. Have you ever heard of Ambien?"

"Believe what you want to believe, Donna. But try as you might, you'll never be able to organize the cosmos and fit them in one of your neat little storage solutions."

I rubbed a hand over my face. "Look, Bella. I had a rough day and I'm meeting with a new client tomorrow. I don't want to argue with you so I'll say thank you for coming to get me and for letting me stay here and good night."

With that, I set my drink aside and made for the stairs before our disagreement escalated.

The way they always did.

Bella

SO STUBBORN. I shook my head as I watched Donna climb the stairs to our old room. There had been a time when the two of us had been inseparable. We'd slept in the same bed, matched our clothes, and couldn't stand being more than a few feet apart.

Then something changed.

If she hadn't been immune, I would have thought a wraith had burrowed deep under her skin, like a tick. Her personality shift had been that drastic. Donna had gone from being fun and outgoing to withdrawn and judgmental. She didn't believe in her own magic or our role as guardians of the portal.

That part hurt almost as much as when she'd asked me to stay out of her life.

The loss of her had been too much. I'd never known loneliness as I had over the last year. No company, no relief from my thoughts or grief or the fever dreams that plagued me night after endless night.

I smoothed a hand over my belly. That was why I'd decided to have these babies. So that I wouldn't be alone forever. The situation wasn't ideal. It had been foolish and impulsive and created even more fear in my heart. But the thought of having children to love and teach excited me too. I only harbored one regret and experience had taught me that regret, while unfortunate, was better than the alternative of not living, not trying, and not striving for what you wanted.

Now Donna was back. Even if she claimed not to believe in fate, I knew that the universe had a hand in her return. I just needed to convince her she should stay. Embrace her destiny.

Axel jogged down the stairs but hesitated in the doorway. After all these months, he could read my mood better than anyone other than Donna. "Is she going to be all right?"

"Her husband is cheating on her," I told him.

His eyebrows went up. "Do you want me to bring you the mirror?"

Out of respect for Donna, I hadn't checked on my brother-in-law or nephew, but such a sudden change of behavior needed to be investigated. I shook my head. "I've got it."

He hesitated and I raised a brow, waiting.

"Anything else?" I quirked a brow.

His gray eyes were guileless. "Just wondering if you're really a legacy witch. You never mentioned it."

Damn Donna for bringing that up to Axel. In an offhanded manner, I shrugged. "Are you really an assistant?"

He nodded as he absorbed that and then flashed me a grin. "I am now. I'll get dinner going."

I moved to the window and stared at my reflection in the leaded glass and thought about the first time I'd seen Axel. His aura had called to me from where he stood, withering behind the bar. And he had been kind.

He wasn't quite human. After one glance I knew that much. His colors were too pure, too clean. Completely untainted. Wraiths couldn't settle on him. Though I'd never used my gift of reflection on him, I recognized his need to come home with me. That it would lead him to his ultimate desire. He didn't know what he longed for and out of respect for someone close to me, I hadn't looked into his mind, his heart, or his background. His secrets were his own.

I'd learned the hard way that sharing your secrets with others gave them the idea that they could unearth yours. My secrets needed to stay buried.

I shook myself out of the fugue state and headed for the mirror. With it, I could locate them all, the faces of those who were lost to the phantoms who served demonkind. The mirror was the wraith's way in as well as the key to their detection.

I scanned the location, but there were no new possessions in Shadow Cove. The portal was safe for now. Maybe I could finally get some sleep.

Of course, I did have that potion to brew for the garden, the one to take care of the aphids. And Donna would need something to wear. And when was the last time I'd showered? I sniffed my armpit and wrinkled my nose. Yeah, a shower was in order.

A gust of otherworldly wind followed me into the first-floor suite room and a sultry southern voice purred, "The prodigal daughter returns then?"

"Annabeth," I turned away from the mirror to face the specter. "Don't start on Donna right away. She's had a rough day."

The teenage poltergeist wore a vintage dress with full voluminous skirts that had either been blue or purple. Her transparent appearance made it hard to distinguish colors. She pouted prettily and twirled her open parasol over her bonnet-covered sausage curls. "You never let me have any fun."

"That's because your idea of fun usually ends up with another body to bury. And my back hurts enough as it is." I put my hands there in illustration.

Annabeth had been at the Sanders house since its construction. No one knew her last name or where she had come from. I knew because I'd once asked our mother why no one had exorcised the girl's spirit and banished her from our realm of existence.

Her answer still haunted me. *Better to have evil up your sleeve than gunning for you.*

Hovering four feet over the thick oriental carpet, Annabeth sashayed around the room. "He's been watching you again." She spoke almost casually.

All the hairs rose along the nape of my neck. I schooled my features though. Showing Annabeth a reaction was like opening a vein in shark-infested waters. "He's back then?"

Her eyes narrowed to slits. "Yes. Should I go spy on him again?"

I weighed the risk and then gave in to temptation. "Since you said he's spying on me, it would only be fair to return the favor, right?"

Annabeth nodded, her sly grin stealing over her doll-like features and then faded from sight.

I swallowed and then braced my hands against the cool glass. How much did he suspect? Would he come here, try to talk to me? Or worse, would he plot and plan, using his wraith-infested minions to strike back at me?

I shut my eyes, sensing the wards around Storm Grove. Nothing with a physical body could cross into the territory without my knowledge. He could send as many spies as he liked but if he tried to come himself, I would be ready.

No one was going to take my children from me. *No one.*

CHAPTER 4
DONNA

T'd forgotten about the bats in the attic. The entry and exit point to the colony's roost was directly above my old bedroom, aka the green room. I lay on my side facing the window, clad in an old robe I'd left in the closet and trying to force my wonky brain into a state of rest when the first flutters sounded. Then the scuffling noises as the cauldron of winged beasties made their way out to hunt for the night.

Normal people would have hired pest control to deal with the bats decades ago. Their droppings could create all sorts of health problems and the little bastards carried thousands of viruses. But not the Sanders family. Grand had installed bat houses in trees all over the property and my mother had always maintained she would rather have bats defecating in our attic than clouds of mosquitos attacking her while she worked in the garden.

Tossing the covers aside, I strode to the window that overlooked my mother's garden. Not much to see in the blue-black nightscape. The crescent moon was hidden behind scudding clouds. A wolf howled in the distance. A moment later, another answered. Bella's strays were still in residence then.

The werewolf bunkhouse was at the far end of Storm Grove from the manor house. That put miles of distance between us and the unfortunate females who'd been forcibly changed. The ones Bella had sought out and saved from male-dominated packs where the women were just another commodity for them to fight over.

My sister did good things with her powers. Necessary things. She just couldn't understand why I wasn't willing to wade into the fray alongside her.

The last time I'd been at the house, the garden had gone to seed, the weeds overtaking what had once been winding rows of herbs and vegetables and flowers. Neither Bella nor I had inherited our mother's green thumb. While I could tell a tomato from a squash once the fruit ripened, everything before that stage looked like a sea of leaves.

Movement below caught my eye. I squinted, having removed my contacts when I lay down. The broad shoulders gave him away as he bent down, digging at something in the earth. Axel.

Another howl in the distance. He didn't even twitch. Axel must be used to the crazy.

My teeth sank into my lower lip as I watched him. Could I blame Bella for shacking up with someone who looked that good? That would be some incredible DNA to work with. Their kids would be glorious.

At that moment he stood from his crouch and looked directly up at my window.

Like a ninny, I jumped to the side and hid behind the curtain. My heart pounded. There was no way he could see me creeping on him, right? I was two stories up and it was dark out.

"Skanky old cougar must run in the family," I muttered and then turned back to bed. Despite my exhaustion, sleep proved elusive. The room was crammed full of boxes and bags, yellowed lampshades, and ugly bric-a-brac. Not like the serene space I'd created at home. A light gray with hints of blue. Blue comforter and fluffy white pillows. A small bedside table for a book, my glasses, and my phone. Maybe a glass of water. The painting I'd had commissioned of a storm rolling in off the ocean and purple lightning streaking in the distance, was the first sight I woke up to every morning.

A perfectly restful space.

Forcing my mind forward, I thought about what I needed to do before I met with my new client the next morning. Get my car and some clothes. There was no way I was showing up to meet with a client in one of Bella's hippy-dippy swooshy patchwork costumes.

I wondered for a moment if I should call Devon. I'd promised him that I would give him his space at college. Besides, what would I say? *Your father changed the locks without telling me and then had me arrested?* Not the kind of thing a mother wanted to dump on her child.

My thoughts skipped around like little kids on a playground until I gave up on sleep altogether, clicked on a light, shuddered at the mess, and did what I did best —brainstormed.

I started with the next day's to-dos. I'd run to

Walmart in the morning and buy myself a temporary wardrobe. Just a few pairs of jeans and shirts until I could get back into the house. Then I should call a lawyer. A pang went through me. Lewis was obviously way ahead of me on that front. But he couldn't just deny me entry to our home, could he?

How long he had been planning the divorce? The timing was too perfect for it to be a spur-of-the-moment decision. At least he'd waited until Devon was out of the house before having his strumpet over.

Or...had he?

I tasted bile at the thought of Lewis sneaking that little piece of naval lint into my home, my bed, while I was out at work. My blood started to boil as I imagined him moving her into the home I'd spent the greater part of my adult life cultivating. Bad enough she was stealing my husband but I'd be damned if she benefited from years of hard work.

A soft knock on the door to my bedroom jerked me out of my dark musings. Clearing my throat I called, "Come in."

The door swung inward. Axel stood there holding a mug. "I saw your light on and thought you could use something hot."

Half a dozen dirty thoughts stampeded through my brain so it took more effort than it should have for me to respond. "That was considerate. Thanks."

He strode in looking like sin on a stick and placed the mug down on the desk beside me. "Bella has a hard time sleeping too."

"It's the age," I told him as I wrapped my fingers

around the mug of what looked to be hot chocolate. "No woman in our age group can get a decent night's sleep without some heavy-duty prescriptions."

He tilted his head and studied me. "How old are you?"

I choked on my cocoa. Axel reached forward and pounded me on the back as I struggled for air.

"Didn't anyone teach you that it's rude to ask a woman her age?" I wheezed.

His stormy gray eyes were guileless as he shook his head. "No. I grew up in foster care. Social etiquette wasn't high on the priority list."

My lips parted. "I'm sorry."

He shrugged. "It wasn't your fault. You weren't the one who abandoned me."

"No, but I'm old enough to be," I pointed out.

He studied me for long enough that I had to fight the urge to squirm. There was more to Bella's PA than I'd thought.

He nodded to my phone. "So what is it you usually do when you can't sleep?"

"Make lists for work. I'm a decluttering and organizing professional."

"Like those people on TV?" Axel raised his brows as though my job impressed him. Which of course it didn't. In my experience, most people, especially young men, didn't see the value in paying someone to help them find efficiencies in their homes. Clutter and inefficiency didn't impact the neurotypical in the same way it did for people prone to anxiety or the neurodivergent.

"Except not so famous as the people on TV," I smiled and then blew on the cocoa.

Instead of yawning or making an excuse the way I'd expected, he pulled an armchair away from the wall so we sat at a 90-degree angle to one another other.

"How did you get into that line of work?" he asked. "Did you go to school for it or something?"

"Nothing so formal," I sighed and sipped my cocoa. "I went to school but only made it two semesters before I dropped out. This is delicious by the way."

Axel smiled and waited.

I took another sip from the mug and decided that I owed him a little insight for being such a judgmental harpy. "I have ADHD."

He blinked but didn't say anything so I set the mug aside and turned to face him. "Being surrounded by clutter makes it worse. Like this place." I gestured to the overly large furniture and jam-packed bookshelf that held everything except books. "My brain doesn't settle well. Sometimes I get so fixated on one thing that I forget to eat or shower. At other times I'm like a horny jackrabbit bouncing from one thing to the next. This place makes it worse."

"How so?" Axel tilted his head in curiosity.

I gestured to the space around me. "You live here and you know how crammed full every room is. My mother and Bella call it the Sander's legacy. I call it the fifth circle of hell. When I lived here, I had to fight to hold a thought from the time I woke up in the morning until I fell into a fitful sleep. I ended up losing myself in projects I never finished or spacing out. Too much stuff leads to me being even more easily distracted. It's like I'm standing in a field and there are dozens of fires all around me and I can't decide which I should put out first. So, I had to learn how much I could deal with."

Axel nodded. "For survival."

Funny, I'd never thought of it in those terms. But he was right. It had been me or the stuff. "Exactly." I reached for the mug again, needing the chocolate boost.

"I'll pull all this out of here," he offered.

I blinked. "Oh, you don't need to bother yourself." I wasn't going to be staying long.

Our eyes met and he reached out and brushed a knuckle across my lower jaw. "Maybe I want to bother."

I quit breathing. Just gave it up in that instant because my lungs had frozen in place. What was Axel saying?

"I'm right across the hall if you need anything." He plucked the mug from my nerveless fingers.

"You are?" That made no sense. Bella's room was on the ground floor. The room across from our old one had been a spare bedroom.

Before I could ask about it though, Axel returned the armchair to the corner and nodded. "Night, Don."

The door shut with a click.

Before I realized what I was doing I was up on my feet and had flung myself at the door. My heart pounded and my hands shook. The old key was the type that stayed in the lock and I turned it with a vicious twist. Then I sagged.

Surely he hadn't meant to come onto me. Maybe Axel was just a flirt by nature. Maybe I was so out of practice that I didn't recognize real flirting from play flirting anymore. He couldn't have been serious. He was with Bella.

Wasn't he?

The sound of male laughter drifted through the door.

I crawled back into bed and shut off the light.

At least he'd given me something to think about other than Lewis the letch.

THE NIGHTMARE always started the same way. The big house that a family had left in a hurry. Able to carry only a few items, they'd abandoned ninety percent of their material possessions.

And I had to deal with it.

Overwhelm threatened. I *hated* this part. The sorting, the lack of systems. Often I'd get distracted by one thing and forget what I was doing. Damn wonky brain.

I had to fix this massive house. Unlike in real life, I couldn't walk away from it, couldn't leave until the job was done. I moved from room to room. Trying to get my bearings, to find something to focus on, something that would help me pick a direction.

The dream blurred then, the way dreams do and the next scene had the top floor of the space finished. I'd removed the unnecessary and was living in the upstairs space. But something was off.

And then I spotted the stairs.

The building was in the city center, right in the middle of everything, and it had been laid out more like apartments than a single-family home. I went downstairs and once again was overwhelmed by the immense amount of stuff. Old-fashioned furniture mixed with modern tech. Personal items and clothes and tchotchke and books, papers, garbage, just stuff. I was being buried under the crushing weight of the never-ending job. *Too much stuff!* My wonky brain screamed as it began to overload. *I can't handle this much stuff! It's suffocating me!*

I woke, gasping. My hands shook as I ran them through my hair, struggling to ground myself in reality. It didn't take a shrink to figure out what the nightmare meant. My need for order wasn't exactly a state secret. Hell, I'd been telling Bella's PA about it. So a dream that I could never achieve the level of organization that I needed to function left me on the verge of a panic attack.

And my surroundings weren't much better. Years of other people's rubbish had been crammed into the space, making me feel like I was just another scratched armoire or a tarnished candle stick. Unwanted detritus no one had bothered dealing with and tucked out of sight. To make somebody else's problem. There was no room to create, to breathe.

Axel said he would clear the space out. While it was sweet of him to offer, that would only mean I was going to stay here long-term. I didn't have any better option at the moment but the thought of moving back in with my sister made me itch.

I knew that life. Had lived on the outer edge of it all through my childhood. The dud who never manifested a root power and therefore couldn't work even the simplest spell. The damaged daughter with a million ideas who flitted from thing to thing, never achieving much because she was too easily distracted. The young woman whose mother hadn't bothered to say goodbye.

It had taken me years to overcome that. Years where it felt like everyone else had received a tutorial in how to do basic shit that I'd missed. Years of developing systems that didn't make sense to anyone but me to combat the chaos of opening my eyes and immediately spinning out. Being Devon's mom gave me a single point to focus on. When he was a baby, I didn't have to choose what to do that day because his needs came first. Always. That tiny human engaged me the way no one and nothing else ever did. He was in my line of sight so I never drifted off like an untethered balloon. His cries brought me back to earth. I learned to care for him first, and myself second because he needed me to find a way to function. I had to show up for him. I had to keep him clean and fed and happy.

Bedtimes, yeah, that wasn't a thing. I didn't nag him about brushing his teeth or taking a shower because that was the kind of shit I forgot to do for myself. But my creativity and enthusiasm for being his mom, for going out and exploring nature, and playing make-believe led to a happy child.

If not a happy spouse.

Lewis did all the drudge work. The cooking, the laundry. "Why are you so lazy?" He'd bitch at me when he didn't have any clean socks. "You're home all day, you think you could handle the washing."

That was Lewis's level of confrontation. Shitty comments. In those days I didn't say anything back. I didn't want him to know my secret. That there was something wrong with me. It wasn't that I didn't want to have clean and neatly folded clothes at the ready for my family. I just...forgot. My brain was on an adventure quest with my son, not fucking around with the vacuum.

Those first five years, where I had been my son's whole world were the best. Time, my constant nemesis, didn't exist. There was only the now, the moment. When I'd watch him sleep or tickle his tummy. Lewis grumbled about the state of the house, but what did it matter? My son was happy and thriving.

And then Devon started kindergarten.

That left me home, surrounded by a shitload of boring ass things to do and no will to do any of them. Cleaning had never been my forte. Let Lewis do it, he liked to have everything just so.

"This place is a sty," he complained one day when he stepped in something sticky. "What do you do all day that you can't mop the floors?"

Shame made my cheeks heat. I'd been working on reupholstering a chair I'd found on the side of the road. Which had led me to the craft store, which led me to the aisle where all the fake flowers were out where I'd run into my friend Vanessa who was getting married and was trying to figure out how to decorate an arch for wedding photos. "So, I offered to do it for her," I summed up. "I found all of these cute ideas on Pinterest and...."

"What's she paying you for this?" I'd watched Lewis's face get redder and redder as I'd explained how my various side quests had led to me being out of the house all day but his question took me aback.

"Paying me?" I shook my head. "I'm not getting any money. Just doing a favor for a friend."

"If you can't keep the house clean, you should get a job," he lectured. "That way we can hire someone to clean."

I blinked at him. A million ideas vied for my attention. I could be a wedding planner!

That one had lasted less than two months. While I liked some aspects, there were so many details. I soon grew bored with the flowers and the color schemes.

Maybe I could be a photographer. I went out and bought a digital camera, the best on the market. Lewis had turned purple when he saw the credit card bill but I'd barely noticed his fit because I'd been busy studying the rule of thirds, the bokeh effect, and golden hour.

Then there'd been my pet grooming business. That had lasted until a German Shepard had nearly taken my arm off. Then yoga instructor, but that was too slow for me and I'd never finished my certification. Career after career, one failed business after the next. Being Devon's mom was the only thing I'd ever been any good at.

It had happened almost by accident.

Lewis had been away at a conference. Devon was on a weekend camping trip with the scouts. I'd been feeling particularly shitty because my house was a wreck and I couldn't find my phone. So I decided to start getting rid of things.

All the things.

I zipped from room to room with a trash bag and a box for donations just discarding it all. The silver lining to my ADHD? While I might give in to impulsiveness, I had no real attachment to things I wasn't using. And I felt...lighter afterward. The house looked better, almost like a hotel. On impulse, I called the number for the cleaning service Lewis had left on the fridge. They came in and took care of dirt, mildew, and all the little nooks and crannies. When they were done I paid them and left, not wanting to fuck up the perfection inside. I walked around the lake, imagining how happy my husband would be to come home to a clean home. It would be a fresh start for both of us.

I met Lewis at the door and watched his face. I'd hoped he would have smiled and taken me in his arms, told me he was proud of me for doing all of this work.

Instead, his eyebrows had pulled together. "Where's my TV?"

"I got rid of it." It came out small, like a squeak.

"You *what?*" His eyes had bulged. "Why would you do that?"

"The mess is gone." I tried to point out the positives. "That whole nest of wires that was

snaking out of the side collecting dust?"

He stared at me for a long minute. "Do you have any idea how much it will cost to replace that television?"

"No, but I can look it up," I headed for my laptop already in research mode.

He gripped my arm. "What is wrong with you?"

I blinked at him, not understanding why he was so upset. Isn't this what he'd wanted? A

clean house? It's all he ever talked about and I knew I'd done a good job. There wasn't a speck of dust anywhere.

45

He'd let me go and then stared at the floor for a long time.

"I'm sorry," I said at last. "I didn't think it was such a big deal. I grew up without a television. I thought we could spend more time together...you know. As a family?"

"Family," Lewis said and then walked away. A moment later I heard a door slam and flinched.

I sat on the couch and stared at the empty wall where the big ugly television had been. Lewis was the one who managed the money. Of course, he was upset that I'd gotten rid of something valuable. But I truly believed I'd done the right thing. We didn't need that stupid television. Or those vases that his great aunt had given us for a wedding present. Or the old bench seat that I hadn't gotten around to staining. Or the ocean of throw pillows that needed to be moved if you wanted to sit on the couch. When Lewis was gone the TV just sat there like a big eyesore. Devon and I preferred to be outside when the weather was good. Hiking, swimming or just hanging out at the neighborhood pool. When it was cold, we read or played video games on the system in his room.

Once upon a time, Lewis had done those things with us. Back then he didn't mind that I couldn't balance a checkbook or even find it. He'd been sure and stable and acted as the anchor that I needed. But then he'd gotten a raise at work and had bought that TV and DVR. When he wasn't at work he was glued to the damn thing. Obviously, he found it more interesting than he found us.

Something inside me broke as I sat on that couch. I

knew I'd never be able to be the wife he wanted. No matter what I did, he was always unhappy. I was tired of feeling like I couldn't get anything right. If I had a better alternative, I'd leave.

But I didn't. My credit rating was garbage. I was unemployed. If I left Lewis, I would have nowhere to take Devon.

Nowhere other than to Bella's.

But no, I wouldn't do that to Devon. I needed to find out the answer to Lewis's question. Find out what was wrong with me.

It had taken six months to get the official diagnosis of ADHD. My hyperfocus let me research the hell out of my symptoms. I didn't share the diagnosis with my husband. I doubted it would change anything. Instead, I asked for his help in starting a new business.

"What is it this time?" Lewis had asked.

"Home organization," I said.

He stared at me. "Is this some sort of joke?"

"Our house is organized isn't it?"

"That's because you got rid of everything!"

I shrugged. "And when was the last time I lost my keys?"

He stared at me for a long minute. "You think you can do this?"

I'd turned toward the wall. "I think I can help people." People like me and my son. I'd do the hard shit, the boring shit, all the things that dragged me down if it meant I made a better life for the two of us. A life where I didn't feel judged, where I had to lock myself in the bathroom to cry.

It hadn't been easy to stick with it on the hard days. I missed chasing the dopamine rush of impulse, of having to rein myself in when someone just wanted a refresh instead of a whole new style. I'd done it for Devon. And I helped people. Women like me who also hadn't gotten the handbook on being the domestic goddess. Eliminate, automate, and delegate. I'd help them simplify and set up systems so they could find the important things and live their lives. And most importantly, I helped them feel good about themselves.

Somewhere along the way I'd forgotten why I'd started. That I wanted to be free and needed to set up a life independent of my passive-aggressive husband.

Now, I didn't have a choice.

I spaced out after that, my mind drifting aimlessly. Goddess, I missed Devon. Missed the sound of his feet thundering down the stairs, the door slamming as he ran to catch a ride with his friends. The massive bear hugs. I could have used his sunshine right about now.

Instead, I was here. In the Sanders house, surrounded by useless crap. The urge to just start pitching it all out the window was strong. Instead, I swung my feet over the side of the bed and headed for the stairs.

I found Bella out on the patio that overlooked the garden. She wore a purple maternity dress with a scooped neckline and fluttery sleeves and enough silver bangles to cover her forearms. Her hair was pulled back into a messy bun and her eyes were lined with kohl. She was tapping away at a laptop, which seemed very high-tech for the Sanders house.

I'd had nothing to put on other than the t-shirt and

jeans I was wearing when I'd been arrested the day before. They stank of mildew and I was delaying getting dressed until the last possible moment so I was still swathed in the threadbare bathrobe.

"I'm not sure if this is good news or not, but there are no wraiths attached to your pant-load of a spouse," she informed me as she shut the laptop.

My gaze fell to her stomach and I hesitated. "May I?"

She made a gesture that indicated I was welcome. I put a hand over the mound in her middle. A smile tugged at the corners of my lips. "You're going to be someone's mom."

"Scary, isn't it?" She grinned back and we shared a moment.

Bella looked away first and then stirred a mug full of foul-smelling liquid.

"Ugh, what is that?" My nose scrunched up at the pungent aroma and I recoiled from touching her. "It smells like a rotting stump."

"It's wood ear and peppermint tea," she said and took a sip. "Good for awakening the third eye, lowering cholesterol, cleansing the liver, and promoting gut health. You should try some."

My nose crinkled in disgust. "Wood ears are mush-rooms aren't they?"

"They don't have much flavor of their own." Bella took a sip.

My stomach rolled at the thought of fungus tea. "I don't have time this morning. I have a new client meeting and need to get home. I was wondering if you could drive me to go pick up my car?"

"Sorry," Bella said. "I have somewhere to be."

"Can't you just drop me on the way?" I asked after a moment when she offered nothing further. Unlike me, Bella didn't see a need to vomit up an explanation whenever somebody inquired. It was why she would always remain the more mysterious twin.

"I can't. Hey, I know. Axel has a car. Maybe he'll drive you."

"No," I sputtered. But it was too late.

"Axel!" Bella shouted through the open terrace doors.

I bit off a groan at the sound of his footsteps, then pasted on a smile before turning to face him.

"Donna needs a ride," Bella stated.

"If it's not too much trouble," I added. "You probably have things to do and I don't want to impose."

"No problem," Axel said easily and set a bowl of fruit salad down in front of my sister. "It's market day and I was heading into town anyway. When did you want to go?"

"As soon as possible."

He frowned as he saw that there was no plate or cup set out next to Bella's place. "You need to eat something first."

"Oh, I'm good."

I'd expected Axel to nod and wander off. He didn't. "You didn't eat anything last night either."

"Really, it's okay. I'm not much of a breakfast person."

"It's the most important meal of the day," Bella piped up.

I bared my teeth at her and gritted out, "I'm fine, thanks. I need to get going."

"I'll meet you out front in ten," Axel said.

Bella speared a piece of cantaloupe as he walked away. "Funny, I didn't think he'd back down that easily. The man is obsessive about feeding me."

"That's because you're eating for three," I pointed out.

"I laid out clothes for you on my bed," she said in an offhand manner. "And before you give me the I'm fine speech, you should know that Axel has your damp duds in the wash. So unless you want to hit downtown Shadow Cove in your robe, you'll need to borrow something."

I sighed. "Thank you."

"Was that so difficult?" Bella winked and speared another bite of fruit.

I hustled through the lower floor until I reached the main bedroom. During Grand's time, the drapes had always been pulled tightly shut. I was surprised to see that Bella had the curtains tied back. They were much lighter fabric than the heavy blackout ones. She'd removed the gaudy wallpaper too and replaced it with warm sand-colored paint. The furniture was the same. Dark heavy pieces and the room was a hot mess explosion of fabric and books and random bottles and bunches of herbs and a variety of crystals. Vintage witch gone wild.

Emphasis on the wild. The bed was unmade and half the decorative pillows were on the floor. My sister had always been a slob, and it had driven me nuts because I could never find anything in her mess.

The dress Bella had laid out for me was draped over the foot of her bed, in a garment bag. I unzipped it and stared. The price tags were still attached. I blinked when I saw the numbers. More than I would have spent on a single article of clothing. But Bella had always been frivolous. The garment seemed a little sedate for her. She typically wore jewel tones but the breezy floral print was much more my speed. It had a v-neckline and cap sleeves and the hem hit me just at the knee. She hadn't put out stockings, but it was too hot for them anyhow. A pair of sandals the color of bone sat in a box at the bottom of the bag. I slipped them on and then turned to survey myself in the large freestanding mirror.

It was an enormous thing that had an alcove of its own. Both Bella and Grand were adamant that no part of the body should be reflected in a mirror while they slept. Supposedly that's how the wraiths got in. Bella had even erected a screen around it to make sure there would be no accidental exposure.

I circled the screen and studied my appearance. Not my usual style but I had to admit, I looked worlds better than I had the day before. My hair was still damp from my shower and the humidity would bring out the worst in the curls if I left it free, but it worked with the look. This was an outfit that would tell both Lewis and my new client that I was a woman who knew how to handle myself.

When I stepped out from behind the screen Bella stood there proffering a necklace. The cord was a parachute string that ended in a net bag. Within the bag was an unpolished, uncut stone that looked either blue or black depending on the way the light hit it.

"No." I crossed my arms over my chest.

"Hematite," she spoke as though she hadn't heard me. "It'll ground and protect you."

"No," I said again. "No crystals, no potions, no mojo bags. Clutter stresses me out."

"It'll help you find your center," Bella insisted. "And it's not clutter, it's jewelry."

I pinched the bridge of my nose. "Bella—"

"Look, you won't let me do anything else," she said. "At least let me do this for you."

When dealing with clients who had a hard time saying no to loved ones who continued to foist unwanted items onto them, I advocated for setting boundaries. Holding the line. But like everything else in life, it was easier said than done.

"Fine." I took the necklace and dropped the cord over my head. "But it clashes with this dress."

Bella's lips curved up. "Didn't you hear? Protection is the new black."

CHAPTER 5
BELLA

I felt as though I could breathe easier once Donna put on the necklace. I'd told her the truth. Hematite was a stone of balance and protection. It was also a stone that helped the wearer release self-imposed limitations. I'd left that bit out because if Donna wanted to pretend she had forgotten everything she'd learned about being a witch, I was willing to play along.

For a while.

Axel had pulled his truck around. I grinned when I saw him shove a brown paper bag into my sister's hands. She scowled at it as though he'd handed her a sack full of night crawlers instead of what I guessed was one of his signature muffins. My assistant loved to bake and had been ridiculously excited because he'd snagged fresh apples at the farmer's market the week before. Donna's willpower didn't stand a chance.

I knew he'd caved too easily earlier. Axel was relent-less, one of the qualities that made him so invaluable as a

PA. He seemed to instinctively understand that it was easier to come at Donna sideways than to clash with her head-on. I would have to remember that.

"Annabeth?" I called out when the truck vanished beyond the gate. The phantom appeared right away, drifting beside me as I walked out into the garden.

"What did you find out?" I asked.

"Nothing. The wards were reinforced. By the time I got through the first of them, the sun was already coming up."

"Damn." The poltergeist was tethered to this house during the daylight hours. At night Annabeth's spirit was free to travel the world but her strength faded in the sun. "He must be there still. No one else could keep you out."

Annabeth yawned prettily and then asked, "My payment?"

"You'll get it when the job is done," I snapped. "Head back over there at sundown."

She bared her teeth at me but without her payment, there was nothing the spirit could do.

She faded from view as I headed for the tree line, lost in thought.

Deep inside my womb, my little passengers stirred. It was such an unnerving experience at first, the quickening of life. Though I'd always assumed I would be the mother to twins, I'd never thought about this part of the process. My body carried them, sheltered them, gave them everything they needed. Or what it was like to be alone and pregnant.

Sure, Axel was with me and there were the wolves. But I craved family.

On impulse, I made my way up the hill to the small cemetery. It sat on a perch of flat ground overlooking the river below. I went to pay respects to Grand first. On and on, back through seven generations of Sanders women, I touched the stones paying homage to each. It was a small ritual that helped me remember all the valiant women who'd come before me, who fought the demons and their wraths, and some of whom, like Grand's twin, had paid the ultimate sacrifice.

"Rest easy, you've earned it," I said to them. The wind blew from the north, a cooling breeze that felt like a caress. My bare feet carried me down the gentle slope that was part of the floodplain for the river. My thinking spot lay dead ahead. It was where I came to sort through a problem, or at the very least center myself so I was prepared to face the challenges ahead of me.

A soft breeze blew the hair back from my face and I drew in a long breath, imagining the air flowing down into my lungs where the oxygen would be filtered into my blood and then given to my girls. My living gave them life. I tried to imagine what they would look like, what they would *be* like. Would they have the same raven dark hair and spooky green eyes as me? Or would they resemble their father?

A shiver ran through me at the thought.

And what about their personalities? Would they be the best of friends the way Donna and I had been when we were young? Or would each pursue her unique interests, growing apart until they no longer resembled one another at all? The way Donna and I were as adults.

The ward sounded an instant before he appeared

beside me. A beautiful man with eyes the color of shadows at midnight and hair black as a raven's wing. His symmetrical features were perfect, his lips full and enticing. His shoulders were broad and he stood several inches over six feet. Almost head and shoulders above me. The whiff of brimstone filled my senses.

Like everything else about him, his appearance was a lie.

His rough voice rasped over my every nerve ending. "You've been spying on me, witchling. Or rather, trying to. I felt your poltergeist bouncing off my wards like a bug in a jar."

I held up a hand, channeling power directly from the ley line beneath me until energy crackled through my veins. It wasn't enough to stop him. No natural force in this world could stop a creature like the one that stood before me.

"Declan," I breathed, speaking his chosen name, not the one I'd used to summon him. "It's my responsibility to know what you're doing."

His glamor shimmered as he circled me. It was an unnerving sensation, to be watched by someone with such...intensity.

"Tell yourself that, witchling." Those lips quirked up. "All you like. But we both know the truth. If you want to know what it is I'm doing, just ask."

I lifted my chin. "What are you doing, then?"

His smile grew even more predatory. "Building an empire."

"Why bother?"

He shrugged. "That's my business."

"I'm your summoner," I reminded him.

Quick as a striking snake he reached out and curled one of those preternaturally long

fingers around my chin, holding me to his devouring gaze. "Yes, and you're looking for a way to send me back before I fulfill my part of the bargain."

I didn't bother to deny it. It had been an act of desperation. I'd been alone and angry at the time and had lashed out impulsively. By the next morning, I'd realized how rash the action had been. And I'd been searching for a way to make it right ever since.

The hand slid down my neck and over my collarbone before continuing down my shoulder, tracing a scalding line of heat as he made his way to my protruding abdomen. A possessive hand over the mound in a touch that was as much a threat as it was a promise.

"And how are my girls today?" he cooed.

Donna

THE APPLE CINNAMON muffin Axel forced on me was next-level amazing. I had gotten out of the habit of eating breakfast most of the time, preferring to get right to work in the mornings after a quick cup of coffee. My mind was sharper when it wasn't bogged down by food, giving me a lean, hungry edge.

Axel listened to my protests and then again pointed out that I had eaten nothing the night before. "You'll pass out in front of your new client."

I retrenched. "Being jounced around inside your truck isn't great for my appetite."

He pulled the truck off the road. We stared at each other.

"For a pretty boy you sure have one hell of a stubborn streak," I grumbled and then withdrew the muffin. It was the size of a softball and smelled strongly of cinnamon and wicked indulgence. There was probably more sugar in the thing than I ate in a week, but after the first bite, I didn't care about anything but having more.

"First booze and now carbs," I muttered when the muffin was gone. "You're kneecapping my diet at every turn."

"Good," he said and then restarted the vehicle. "You don't need to diet."

I snorted. "My doctor would disagree."

I'd reached that midlife weight gain phase. It was, to put it mildly, a rabid bitch. Every time I went to his office, Doctor Harris would suggest that it would be better for my health if I 'thought about losing a few pounds.'

Thinking, I could do. The actual losing part...not so much. It didn't matter what went in my mouth or how many hours a week I exercised. The numbers kept on creeping up.

An image of Mindy's taut body covered with whipped cream flashed through my mind. I'd bet my left boob her doctor wasn't telling her to lose weight.

"Your doctor sounds like an asshole," Axel murmured. "Maybe you should get a new one."

He made it sound easy. Like people got new doctors every day. And I guess some people did. But I was a creature of habit. Set in my ways. I stuck to them like gum to a shoe because it minimized impulsive behavior.

"Maybe. Take a left at the stop sign."

Axel didn't press and followed my directions. "So, you said you're meeting a new client today. What does that entail?"

"Depends. Everyone's needs are different. I like to talk with the client and then do a walk-through of the home and come up with a plan of attack."

He flashed me a grin. "You sound like a general planning a siege."

I grinned back. "It is a war. A war on clutter and excess and all the things wrong with modern society. And we're losing."

Axel shook his head. "So much passion. You must be great at it."

I flushed to my black and white roots, pleased. I liked the way this kid saw the world. Saw me.

"Is this the turn?" he muttered.

"Yup." We had reached my street. My Impala was parked in the driveway where I'd abandoned it the day before. The sight of it sitting there, lonely and dejected, burst the little bubble of happiness talking to him had constructed.

Axel was cute and flirty and sweet. But he wasn't real. The reality was Lewis and the twink assistant he was boffing. The divorce looming over my head.

Reality could eat a dick.

"You're doing a lot of sighing over there," Axel observed. "Do you want me to come in with you?"

Slowly, I shook my head. "No, this is something I

need to do by myself." My fingers wrapped around the handle and I opened the door, braced for the next hit. Would Lewis even be at home? He was usually at work by nine and it was twenty after.

A hand reached out and wrapped around my wrist with gentle pressure. "What's your phone number?"

Surprised, I rattled it off. He released me and withdrew his phone from his jeans. A moment later mine vibrated with an incoming message.

I raised my brows at him then flipped my phone over so I could read the message.

Unknown: Text me if you need anything.

"You're my sister's assistant," I reminded him. "You should be worried about helping her, not wading into my mess."

Soft gray eyes met mine. "I don't go where I'm not wanted. Unless I'm needed. Call if you need anything."

And with those cryptic words chasing me, I exited the truck.

Taking a deep breath, I headed up the walkway to the front door where the ugly new lock waited. I didn't bother to try it, not wanting a repeat of yesterday. Instead, I banged on the door until it rattled in the frame.

A moment later Lewis opened it. We stared at each other for a beat.

When was the last time I'd looked at him? Really looked? He had become just part of the background in a lot of ways. Something that was always there, not a positive or a negative, just a constant.

He'd aged visibly when I had been busy raising our son and building a business. His hair had thinned and his waistline thickened. He'd picked up a gym membership about a year ago. I'd thought that was a good sign, that he wanted to take better care of himself. In retrospect, he'd probably been trying to impress little Miss whipped cream tits.

"What are you doing here, Donna?" he asked.

I sucked air between my teeth. "This is my home."

He shifted from foot to foot, clearly uncomfortable. "I told you yesterday—"

"That you want a divorce. Yeah, I heard you. That doesn't change the fact that I've agreed to nothing yet."

I tried to push past him but he blocked me, shutting the door so I couldn't go inside.

A flash of rage washed through me. "She's still here?"

"Mindy's apartment is being fumigated," he said. "She has nowhere else to go."

My jaw dropped at the betrayal. "So, you moved her into *my* house? The one I pay for every frigging month?"

He lifted his chin. "Your name isn't on the mortgage."

Unbelievable. "That doesn't change the fact that this is *my* house. Get your chippie a freaking hotel room."

His nostrils flared, making him look like a pasty bull. "You never took care of the house. You were too much of a lazy ditz to do any maintenance. Is it any wonder I took up with someone else?"

I was so damn angry I couldn't see straight. "No, you are not going to turn this around on me, you slimy little bastard. You're doing this to hurt me. I've been a devoted wife and mother. What the hell did I ever do to you, anyway?"

He laughed and it was tinged with bitterness. "Devoted? You? You spend more time with total strangers than me."

"Maybe that's because total strangers don't call me names or tell me I'm lazy or stupid." I snapped.

"Face facts, Donna. You're a mess, just like your wreck of a sister."

"Don't you dare talk about my sister," I said in a low, warning tone.

He made a scoffing sound. "Two peas in a pod, as usual. You like to pretend you're normal, Donna, but the truth is you're just as much of a freak as she is."

If there was an emotion that bypassed wrath, that sank its talons into your soul and yanked something loose, that was the one coursing through me. I felt the breaking coming from within. Not my heart. Lewis hadn't possessed that in a long time. But my trust in him.

And something else. Something completely foreign and at the same time, completely natural.

"What goes around, comes around, Lewis." Despite my fury, the words came out low and succinct. A warning.

"What does that even mean?" he asked as he took a step back.

Or tried to.

His back hit something solid. Something invisible. His eyebrows drew together and he turned, looking like nothing more than a mime in a box as he felt his way along the invisible barrier. "What the hell did you do?"

"I didn't—" I began, the protest automatic.

"You crazy bitch!" Gone was the chickenshit who avoided confrontation. I saw the vein that bulged in his forehead as he whirled to face me, eyes wide and panicked. He lunged forward, as though to grab hold of me but his hands bounced off another invisible wall. "Let me out of here!"

My hand trembled as I raised it and laid it on the barrier. It was cool to the touch, smooth as glass. But thicker, more impenetrable. Like a hardened wall of air. Lewis banged a fist against it and then let out a vicious curse.

I ran to my Impala and got behind the wheel. My heart thudded in my ribcage as Lewis screamed at me to come back, to let him out as though I had the power to do anything.

As though *I* could wield magic.

But that was impossible. I was a dud. No powers for me. I had certainly never worked a spell that could trap someone. Had never even thought to do so.

But it had happened. I had felt the barrier myself. Unless I was losing my wonky mind, I had worked magic.

No, it was impossible.

My fingers fumbled for the stone necklace. Of course. Bella must have bespelled the thing. That was why she had been so insistent that I take the stone. It was the only logical explanation.

Both my feet slammed on the brakes. The Impala fishtailed before it skidded to a stop in the middle of the road. Behind me, a horn blared and then a Nissan roared past me. I ripped the cord free from my neck, rolled down the window, and dropped it onto the road. Then I put the car in gear. A satisfying crunch filled my ears. I slammed the car into reverse and then backed up to make sure the Hematite stone was pulverized.

Only then did my breathing slow back to something approaching normal. I didn't care if Lewis ever got out of that box. I did very much care that my twin had used her magic on me.

Some sins were unforgivable.

CHAPTER 6

DONNA

O ut of sight out of mind. With ADHD it's more than just a saying. I forgot about Lewis after I left our development. My task was to make a positive impression on my new client, Ali Smith. Nothing else mattered right now. Not Bella and her BS, not Lewis, and definitely not the weirdness of him being locked in an invisible box like some sort of middle-aged mime.

The only problem was, my wonky brain had struck again.

"Fuck," I mumbled as I cruised down the street for the fifth time, looking for my client's house. "Fuck, fuck, fuckity fuck!"

Was I even in the right neighborhood? I didn't know this side of town well. That was a problem. Directional dyslexia was the technical term. To put it bluntly, I got lost a lot.

Shame washed through me. I should have run the route the day before. I tried to do that when I had the chance just so I wouldn't show up late. Overload threatened as my nervous system kicked in and I fought tears.

Okay, Donna. Breathe. You just need to breathe.

Out of the blue, my phone rang. I sniffled and then pulled over. *Axel,* the display read.

"Hey, Don. Do you like artichokes? I was thinking—"

"Axel," I whispered, feeling like a total loser. This was my goddess damned town that I'd lived in my entire goddess-forsaken life. Why couldn't I find one stupid address?

"What's wrong?" His tone sharpened. "Are you all right?"

"I'm lost." It was a little girl's voice that whispered the sad sorry truth.

Axel didn't call me an idiot. Instead he asked, "Is your location on? I can come to you."

"I need to find a client's house. The address isn't coming up on GPS." Had I typed it in wrong? Technology and I didn't mix even on the best days.

His raspy voice filled me with reassurance. "We'll figure it out. I'll be there soon."

He hung up and I sat and tried to focus on my breathing. Inhale for four seconds, out on a six-count. That was my only job for the moment. To take one breath. And another. And another. It kept the overwhelm from setting in. My lip trembled. I sank my teeth into the flesh until I tasted blood. ADHD overwhelm circled like a buzzard ready to pick at my frazzled carcass.

A knock on my window made me jump, There was Axel, grinning down at me. "We've got to stop meeting like this."

I burst into tears.

"Hey, it's okay." He opened the car door and then reached around me and unbuckled my seatbelt. I fell into his arms and he held me there in the middle of the street.

"It's all right," he breathed into my hair. "I've got you."

And he did. I was safe to fall apart. On an instinctive level, I knew I could go to pieces because Axel would hold me until I fit myself back together.

Slowly, the panic abated. I could draw deeper breaths. Embarrassment and shame, my two constant companions, coursed through me. I sat back and wiped my eyes. "I'm sorry."

"Nothing to be sorry for, Don. Tell me what you need."

He made it so simple. So honest. No irritation that I'd gotten turned around. Just straightforward problem-solving. I rose and fumbled in my pocket, praying I hadn't somehow lost the scrap of paper with the address I was trying to find. "This is where I'm supposed to be."

Axel looked at the address, then pulled out his phone and typed something in. "Okay, I think I've got it. We're close. Do you want to follow me there?"

Like a baby duckling heading to the pond for the first time? Not really. But I wasn't about to risk another mishap. "Please."

His warm calloused hand slid over mine. "You've been having a rough week, babe. No worries, I've got your back."

I watched him head back to his truck and then scrambled to secure myself behind the wheel of my

Impala. He made a three-point turn and then slowly headed in the direction I'd been going. He made a left and then a quick right before pulling up to the curb. I navigated in behind him and stared.

A duplex. That was what had messed me up. I let out a shaky sigh.

Axel rolled down the window. "You okay?"

"Just feeling stupid," I admitted. "You made that look so easy."

"None of that, now," Axel murmured. "I'll see you later."

I watched him drive off. He had no idea how much he had saved me. Even though I was behind schedule, I took another minute to compose myself and review the client file.

Ali Smith was a widow in her seventies and entering that phase of life where having too many things around could result in serious medical complications. Ali wanted me to help her declutter and organize so that her sister could move in with her.

A little thrill shot through me as it always did when I saw a client's home for the first time. I never knew what I would be walking into. How people conducted themselves in the outside world rarely reflected on how they kept their homes. The most well-put-together people often had the messiest spaces. I always felt like I was one of the chosen few who got a peek behind the curtain into how someone's brain worked when I saw their space for the first time.

I checked my reflection in the rearview, took a deep

breath, and exited the car before walking up the left walkway to Ali's side of the building.

Her front lawn was tiny and mowed. A positive sign. I had been on a few jobs where the amount of stuff had spilled out of the house and onto the front lawn, resulting in code enforcement coming into the mix. Then there were threats and deadlines and fear, all of which made my job more difficult. People got attached to their possessions. Getting them to see that getting rid of an old lamp or a dusty oil painting didn't diminish them in any way was a big part of why I'd chosen my line of work.

Ali opened the door at my first knock. Her silvery curls were styled neatly and her black sweater and slacks looked freshly pressed. Behind her, I could see the stairs that led up to the second floor and a lone half-moon table with a vase of dried cattails on top of a doily. No piles of mail or baskets of laundry. I was a little disappointed. She seemed more together than I would have expected from someone who wanted to work with a home organizer.

"Are you Donna?" Her voice was thick with southern honey even if it creaked a bit with age.

"That's right." I extended a hand which she took and shook lightly. "It's very nice to finally meet you, Ms. Smith. I apologize for being late, I got a little lost."

"No worries, dear. Please, call me Ali. Won't you come in?"

I crossed the threshold and surveyed the space. Dated, sure but neat as a pin. Maybe Ali was the sort that stashed her clutter in closets and behind closed doors?

"I picked up some sticky buns at the bakery this morning. Would you care for a cup of coffee and a snack?" she asked.

"Sure." The meet and greet was a big part of the process. Breaking bread was a ritual for a reason. Sharing a meal with someone invited intimacy and a chance to reveal hidden truths. Though the last thing my ass needed was more baked goods shellacked onto it.

The kitchen/ dining area was dated but tidy. Ali had a china cabinet that matched her oval table. The wood of the dining table gleamed as though it had just been polished. The kitchen was a galley sort with a pass-through window. From my vantage point, I couldn't see any excessive gadgets or things that obviously didn't belong in a kitchen.

While Ali fixed the coffee, I crept farther down the hall to the living area and sighed. More antique wood, and more doilies, but everything had a home. Out of curiosity, I opened the door to what I assumed was the hall closet. Neat stacks of folded towels, washcloths, and sheets. No hidden hoard of unfinished projects, or secret shame.

What on earth could I even do for this woman?

I'd taken a seat at the dining room table when Ali returned carrying a silver tray with a French press coffee pot and the promised sticky buns. I waited while she settled herself across the table and poured the coffee for both of us.

"So, tell me how I can help you, Ali?" I asked.

She shrugged. "Well, you see, it's my playroom."

I blinked. "Playroom? Like for children or grandchildren?" I hadn't seen any signs of toys.

"No, dear. For adults. Like you read about in those books." A little giggle. "Of course, I got into the lifestyle when I was about your age. I became quite the authority long before those dirty stories became so popular." There was a twinkle in her blue eyes as she said this last bit.

My lips parted but I didn't know how to respond.

Ali continued. "I stayed in the game longer than most. I was never a collector before but each new purchase felt so exciting...I'm afraid it's a bit massive."

"Your collection of sex toys," I croaked.

She nodded. "And now that I'm past my prime, I don't know what to do with it all. Shame to let it all just sit there going to waste. And I need to get it out of here before my sister moves in. She's something of a pearl-clutcher if you get my meaning. Full of tight-lipped disapproval."

How bad could it be? Maybe she was overreacting. "Would you be willing to...er...show me this playroom?"

"Of course. It's downstairs." She popped up like a jack-in-the-box, full of eagerness. I'd seen the same sort of giddy reaction from music lovers who had shown me their massive record collection or bookworms who aspired to fill their home to the rafters with tomes it would take three lifetimes to read. Collectors were often proud of their hoard and eager to show it off.

Nothing could have prepared me for Ali Smith's basement though.

"My husband built this," she said as she gestured to

the wall at the bottom of the stairs. "He was a hell of a carpenter."

A door had been cut into the wall and it stood open. Feeling a little like Alice following the white rabbit, I trailed after my would-be client into the dimly lit space.

Unlike the outside which had been nothing but two-by-fours and sheetrock, the interior walls of Ali's play-room were a muted gray and padded. Soundproof, I concluded when I spied the same material on the ceiling. Another door, also padded, stood directly across from where we had entered. There was no natural light in the space, considering the layout of the house. I guessed that it led to the outside.

The entire space couldn't have been more than fifteen by twenty feet yet the high ceilings gave it the appearance of being much larger. To my left, a black lacquered X made of wood had been fastened to the padded wall. Metal cuffs gleamed in the recessed lighting.

"The bulbs change color. I can do it from my phone." Ali chirped and withdrew her cell. A moment later the color shifted from pale gray to crimson red making the cuffs look even more sinister.

About two feet away from the X was an antique steamer trunk that had also been padded. A series of chains snaked around the top.

"This was my grandfather's. He brought it when he immigrated here. I just love repurposing old things. It's great for storage, too." Ali beamed.

I made some sort of sound though I would have been hard-pressed to categorize it.

Large hooks hung from the wall beside the door. Several were empty but others held lengths of natural fiber ropes, more chains, or whips. My mind couldn't process it all. There were antique dressers and wardrobes in the far corner and I made my way over to inspect the contents.

"That is a lot of dildos." I choked out.

"Well, we wanted to be sure we had enough," Ali said. "And there are always terrific sales after Valentine's Day, where you can get toys half off."

My mind could not for the life of me picture Ali Smith using any of this stuff. Or having it used on her. For once I didn't think my wonky brain was the culprit.

"I can see I've shocked you, dear."

I shut the drawer and turned to face her. "I'd tell you you haven't but we both know I'd be lying."

Ali smiled but it was a sad smile. "It was never my intention to get old. It just sort of snuck up on me. When I went through the change, something sort of...broke loose inside me. It was like I'd been playing a game by a set of rules that someone else had given me. Rules that kept me contained. Made me safe for everyone else to interact with. And it killed a little bit of my soul."

She could have been talking about me. Not the job. But the drudgery....

She took a deep breath. "I quit my job. I was a secretary at the time. And my husband, Henry, asked me what I was going to do with myself. I told him I would start a business from home. And then I came across this article about how certain men paid for certain things. Women bossing them around in the bedroom. I always had a bit of a bossy streak and thought I would be good at it. So, I tried it out. First with Henry to see if I could pull it off. I took to the lifestyle like a duck to water. My husband, well, he started looking at me like I was a new woman. It took both of us by surprise. After our daughter moved out, it breathed fresh air into our marriage."

Even though it was hard for me to imagine, the space was a labor of love. The tender expression on Ali's face was enough to break my heart.

"You had sex with other men?" I cringed as the question passed my lips.

She looked shocked. "Oh no, dear. That was a line neither of us wanted to cross. But I did things to other men. Men who paid for the privilege. You know I have the worst case of tennis elbow my doctor has ever seen? All from countless spankings." A chuckle escaped. "Like I said old age snuck up on me. And without Henry, it's not as much fun as it used to be."

We were both silent for a long moment.

"What," I cleared my throat and tried again. "What do you envision this space to be without...all of this, stuff?"

Her penciled-on eyebrows drew together. "I'm not sure I follow."

"You said you want it gone before your sister moves in. Is this going to be her room?"

"Oh no, dear. Tippy has trouble with the stairs. She'll take my daughter's old room. I just need this all buttoned up first."

She sounded sad at the loss. It was common among people who were transitioning to a different phase of life to want to cling. I needed Ali excited about this or she would never be willing to do the work.

"Well, we should think about converting it into something else. A guest room maybe? With the separate door, you could easily set it up as a rental. Find another way for the space to provide income. One that will be a little easier on your joints."

"Huh," she nodded. "I never thought of that."

"Okay." Once I moved past the purpose, it was a job like any other. "First thing we need to deal with is the sanitary issue. Anything that has been inside a human body needs to be tossed. No ifs, ands, or butts. Especially the butts." I pointed at the wardrobe that I wouldn't be touching again without gloves and gallons of hand sanitizer.

She nodded. "There are a lot of things that are still in the packaging though."

I drummed my fingers on the wooden X. "We can try to sell it in lots."

"The internet?" Ali asked skeptically.

I nodded. "I'll factor in shipping and we'll come up with a price that will help offset the cost of redecorating the space." I'd have to do a little research about the rules. Selling sex toys wasn't something I did every day. "Same with any of the furniture or, er…equipment, that is too big to ship. I'll list it on Craigslist and see if we can get someone to haul it away and pay for the privilege."

Ali laughed. "I like the way you think, Donna."

We made our way upstairs. I started making lists. Much of the furniture could be repainted and repurposed. My buddy Zack was an expert at doing that sort of thing. The space was climate controlled and there was a small powder room that could use a bit of updating.

By the time I finished discussing the possibilities with Ali, it was already past noon. "Uh oh, I better get going. I'll do some research then write up a proposal and get it to you by the end of the week."

"Sounds good." Ali moved her dentures around in her mouth. "Um and Donna...."

I covered my lips with a finger. "I saw nothing." Then I winked at her.

She grinned. "Thanks, I would hate for any of this to get back to Tippy."

I collected my things and circled the duplex to get back to my car.

Before starting the car I checked my phone. There was a missed call from Lewis. My molars ground together. He could just wait. There was also one from Devon.

"Hey, Mom. Could you send me some of those granola bars I like? The ones with the chocolate chips. I don't have time to hit the cafeteria before my eight o'clock class. Kay, thanks. Bye."

I pinched the bridge of my nose. Devon knew all my passwords. There was no reason he couldn't order the bars himself. It was just easier for him to do what he had always done and ask me to do it for him. Of course, it was my own damn fault. I'd been fussing over him since the day he was born. Just this one time, I'd place the order.

I had just clicked checkout on my phone when it rang in my hand.

"Hello?"

"It's me," Bella said. "I need your help."

I pinched the bridge of my nose. "Now isn't a good—"

"One of the werewolves was attacked," Bella said. "She shifted and now she's on the loose. I need you to help me find her before she does something...irredeemable."

Like killing someone. Or changing them. Yeah, I didn't want a Lycan epidemic in downtown Shadow Cove on my conscience.

"You owe me," Bella pushed.

"Fine," I huffed. "Tell me where to meet you. I'll be there as soon as I can."

"I'm at the bunkhouse. And Donna. Please hurry."

CHAPTER 7
BELLA

I stared in disgust at the wraith-ridden man at my feet. The spirit inside hadn't been born to that body—it had dug in like a tick. One I couldn't squish. That was the problem with wraiths. They couldn't be destroyed, merely contained. Essentially people became their human shield. If the being died while housing a wraith, the demonic spirit would simply move on to another victim.

"I don't know what happened." It was Kendra, the woman who ran the bunkhouse for me. She was a few years older than me and Donna. Her head was shaved, entirely but she had one of those perfectly symmetrical skulls so the look worked against her warm brown skin. While I wouldn't say we were friends, we had known each other for a long time. Ever since the night the man Kendra had called over to repair a leaky faucet attacked her in her home.

Single women were often targeted by unscrupulous packs. Especially ones who could disappear. A scout would find the victim, wait for an opportunity, then let the beast loose. If the intended prey survived the change, she was collected by the pack and forced to live with those who'd ruined her life.

It was a hell of an adjustment. The monsters were real. All the things that go bump in the night were more than just stories.

My mother and grandmother used to scour newspapers looking for people like Kendra. There was no reversing the change. A victim who survived an attack shouldn't have to live with the pack who'd changed her. Or be forced into mating with those unscrupulous wolves.

Long before my time, the Sanders women had set up the bunkhouse as a sanctuary for forcibly changed werewolves. A safe place where they could learn what they were and try to build some sort of life independent of a pack. Currently, it housed fifteen werewolves, though we could have sheltered twice as many. It was enough for me to combat the wraiths. I didn't have the time to look for more.

"It's not your fault," I said to Kendra as I looked down at the man. "Did he have any ID on him?"

She nodded and then reached into her back pocket and handed me a leather wallet.

"Austin Brown," I read. "Address says Florida."

"Maybe he's here on vacation," Kendra suggested.

That was a possibility. At any given time, it seemed as though half the state of Florida migrated to the high country of North Carolina to experience the changing seasons and fresh mountain air. I wished they cleaned up after their damn dogs before they headed home though. More than one pair of suede boots had been DNR after tourist season ended.

"The wraith might have brought him here specifically." I had a friend who worked for Florida's department of law enforcement, aka, FDLE. "I'll call Anthony and find out if the guy has been reported missing." Or if he had a record.

Wraiths sometimes chose hosts with criminal backgrounds. Humans who were more prone to violence. I had no idea if these selections were deliberate on the part of the demons who sent the wraiths over. Anyone who slept with their body visible in a mirror could be taken, unless they had preternatural blood that would fight the possession. Witches, both legacy and hedge, weres, shifters, and other supes were immune.

The sound of gravel crunching under tires made us look up from our silent contemplation. A moment later, Donna's silver Impala came into view. I wasn't sure until that moment that she would come but I was glad she did. We needed all the help we could get.

"Is that your sister?" Kendra's pencil-thin eyebrows pulled together. "She looks different than the last time I saw her."

"That's because, unlike some people, we age," I teased. It fell a little flat, with the ensnared man still unconscious on the floor.

Donna emerged from her car. The hemline of the sundress swished about her calves as she walked. I bought it while on a drunken online shopping spree.

Seeing it on her made me certain that it had been meant for my strait-laced sister all along.

Donna pushed her sunglasses up on top of her head. Her green eyes grew wide as she stared at the man on the floor. "Is he dead?"

"No, just possessed."

She ignored that. "You said he attacked someone? Did you call the police?"

No, and I wouldn't, at least not the way she meant. Turning a wraith-ridden person over to the police only delayed the inevitable. I always imagined that the soul of the person whose body had been hijacked was inside, screaming for help. But Donna didn't know these ugly little details about what I did. Grand had said she ought to be protected, at least until she came into her powers. "I was just about to."

"I can do that," Kendra offered. "It's been a while since I talked to Anthony."

Despite the grim situation, I smiled. "Say hi for me." The two of them had a long-distance flirt-mance. That was all it would ever be since Anthony was human and Kendra wasn't.

"Who is the wolf we're looking for?" Donna asked me when Kendra left.

"Her name is Joseline Hayes. She's thirteen years old, and has only been here for a few weeks."

"A child?" Donna stared down at the unconscious man. "Did he rape her?"

The word made me flinch. "He tried. She shifted and ran. Yvette, another recent addition, heard the commotion and came out here brandishing a cast iron skillet.

She saw Joseline just as she disappeared into those trees." I gestured to the pine grove.

"Toward town you mean," Donna sighed. "Does anyone have a recent picture of Joseline? One we could maybe spread around to the searchers?"

"Donna, we are the searchers. You, me, Axel, and the weres."

"Axel?" She repeated and tucked a strand of hair behind her ear.

And wasn't that interesting? "Yes, well he is my assistant. And I need assistance."

She hesitated. "Okay. Where do you want me?"

Donna

"This is pointless." I growled as I stood shivering in front of what Bella and our mother and grandmother had referred to as "the portal." In reality, it was a stone slab about ten feet by ten feet buried beneath the forest floor. If not for the fact no small trees sprouted up from the ground where the stone lay, there would be no distinguishing it from any other spot in the woods.

"One of us needs to guard the portal," Bella had insisted.

There was no sense arguing with her over the slab of stone. It was in the same direction Joseline had run and she might show up here.

"How will I know if it's her if I don't have a picture?" I had asked.

"A picture won't do you any good. She's a werewolf, remember?"

"Well, how can I tell if it's her or a real wolf?" That was a possibility. The weres drove any strays they found out of their territory as a matter of course. But the Storm Grove estate was massive and there was a lot of ground to cover.

Another sharp gust of wind off the river had me wrapping my arms around myself. Another storm was brewing. Out in the sun, my borrowed dress was perfect for the August day. But beneath the heavy-limbed pines, it was another matter.

"Guard the portal," I huffed and scowled at the patch of ground where the stone lay. Feed Bella's delusion was more like it. I thought back to the day a year ago when I'd offered to get her help. Grand had died the winter before and Bella was all alone in her off-putting gothic monstrosity. Even though we'd grown apart over the years, she was still my sister.

"I'll pay for therapy," I'd offered as we strolled the grounds together. "Really, Bella. It's not safe for you to cling to this delusion forever."

"I'm not the one who's fooling herself." Bella's chin had lifted. "You have a destiny. Just because you're choosing to ignore it doesn't mean it isn't real."

I'd rehearsed the speech over and over in my mind. It had been important that I get the words just right, to make her see reason. "Bella, I want you to be happy. Living like this isn't normal or healthy. You're all alone up here, lost in this fantasy where you are in charge of saving the world. You can be doing so much more with your life."

She had said nothing, staring out at the winding water below.

"I think...I think maybe Grand was sick. Like mentally ill. And I think Mom went along with her because it was easier. And that's why she left."

Her eyes had been full of tears when she turned to face me. "Our mother didn't leave us by choice! She was taken. We have gifts, Donna. A purpose. We're supposed to be doing this together."

I'd thrown my hands up in the air. "I have a son. A husband. A business. My life is full. And you want me to just give it all up and come back here so I can play make-believe with you? Don't you care about what I want? What's best for me? This place, it makes me sick, Bella. Physically ill. Coming here brings out the worst in me."

"Then maybe you shouldn't come," she'd whispered. "If I'm so toxic."

I'd wanted to cry. It wasn't her that damaged me, just the heavy yolk of the legacy. But it had dawned on me that I would never be able to accept one without the other. That her belief in her destiny was a crushing weight that would crush me, too, if I let it.

"Maybe I shouldn't," I whispered.

I'd left her standing there, in the family graveyard, surrounded by ghosts. If I could only save one of us, it had to be me.

For a year, I'd gone about my life and everything had been... well, not fine. Obviously. When your husband of twenty years locks you out of the house it's a pretty strong signal that all isn't hunky-dory. But I still knew I'd done what was best for me, for Devon, and even for Bella.

"So why am I standing here, in front of this stupid hunk of rock, talking to myself?" I asked the trees. They didn't answer, which made me feel even nuttier.

I'd almost convinced myself that I should up and leave when my phone rang. Lewis again. He'd been blowing up my phone all afternoon. After our altercation this morning, I highly doubted that he was calling to reconcile. Still, we had things that we needed to work through. Decisions had to be made. I should at least try to be civil.

I answered with, "Lewis, now isn't a good—"

"What did you do, you crazy bitch!?!"

The voice was shrill but familiar. Ah yes, Mindy of the dairy fetish.

"What did I do?" I asked. "I'm not the one sleeping with another woman's husband or stealing her home."

"You trapped him with one of your witchy spells."

Gooseflesh rose along my arms. "What are you talking about?"

"He's been trapped outside by this...this..." She struggled for a word and finally settled on "This hex. I know it was you. I saw you leave."

Bella's spell hadn't faded? That was...atypical. Usually, her magic lasted only long enough to suit her purposes.

A branch snapped behind me. I whirled around. My breath caught at the sight.

"You've got to fix this!" the hysterical woman was shouting.

"Look, Mandy—,"

"It's Mindy. And just because you're a jealous old hag doesn't mean you get to do whatever you want to people."

I stared at the wolf, at the yellow eyes that peered out of the darkness.

"Now isn't a good time," I said into the phone.

"But he'll starve in there!"

I was more worried about ending up as a meal than my overweight ex starving to death after a few hours trapped in an invisible box. "If I live through the next few hours, I'll see what can be done."

I hung up before she could respond and focused all my attention on the wolf.

"Joseline?" I asked warily.

A low growl filled the space between us. I swallowed hard and put out my hands. Living at Storm Grove meant that I'd been taught from an early age how to read canine body language. For survival.

"Never run from a predator." Grand had said with a stern warning in her voice as she lectured the two of us. "Drop your gaze so you don't inadvertently start a dominance contest. Staring, shifting weight forward, ears being pinned back are all signs that the animal is thinking about attacking."

"But they're people," Bella had protested. "That's what you and Mom said. Aren't they?"

Grand had nodded. "They are but when the wolf is ascendent, the animal's instincts override logic and reason. It takes years for a werewolf to learn how to strike a balance between the human being and the animal."

When I'd made a soft whimpering sound Grand had turned her basilisk's gaze on me. "They aren't monsters, Donna. Though some might not believe that at first. But you should always be cautious with a predator. Especially one that doesn't know what they are capable of."

Bella had said Joseline had been at the bunkhouse for a few weeks. That meant very recently turned. Odds were she had little control, especially in light of the most recent attack.

Animals that felt threatened were the most dangerous.

"Hey," I said in a soft voice. "Joseline, it's all right. The man that tried to hurt you is unconscious. The police are coming for him. You're safe."

My reassurance did nothing. She crouched low, preparing to spring.

I eyed the distance between myself and the Impala. Too far. If I ran, she'd go for my throat. She would feel sorry about it later. That was the greatest burden the wolves faced. Dealing with the consequences the beast had wrought.

A fat lot of good it would do me since I'd be dead.

Before I could track it, the wolf surged forward. I shrieked and ran, all training forgotten as the adrenaline kicked in. The car was only a few dozen yards away in the clearing. *Almost there....*

My sandal-shod foot landed in a divot of mossy ground. The bad step pitched me off balance. There was a loud crack followed by a flare of white-hot pain. My phone flew from my hand as I hit the pine needle and leaf-strewn ground as the damaged leg gave out.

It took me a moment to realize that the wolf hadn't sunk her teeth into my ankle. That I'd twisted it when I hit the ground and most likely snapped the bone. The wolf had...run past me?

And run straight for the man who stood not five feet from the leaf-covered stone. He had a knife in one hand. His gaze was vacant. His clothes were torn and ragged as though he'd been living rough for a while. A tweaker most likely. Meth was a big problem in the area.

Exactly what this situation didn't need.

I expected him to strike at the wolf with his weapon. Instead, he flipped it and turned it on his wrist, slicing open a vein.

"No!" I cried out in horror.

The stranger ignored me as though I wasn't there. His sightless gaze went distant. He switched the blade to the bleeding hand and made another slash on the opposite wrist. The wolf hit him with her full body weight and they went down in a tangle of limbs and fur.

Right onto the stone.

The ground beneath us began to quake. Behind me, I heard car doors slamming and more wolves emerging from the trees. Bella ran for me. "Are you hurt?"

"Just my ankle," I panted through the pain.

Then her gaze flew to the struggling pair, the bleeding man. "No!" she shrieked. "Get them off the stone!"

The wolves circled the stone, weight shifted as

though ready to spring. They didn't though. The tremors intensified.

"Axel!" Bella shouted. "Get her out of there!"

"On it." The words came from behind me. Then there was a blur, and suddenly, Axel stood on the far side of the stone, holding the small wolf by the scruff of her neck.

"How...?" I blinked. I hadn't seen him move. One second the wolf was on the stone, the next she'd been pulled away.

"Give me your hand, Donna," Bella commanded.

"Why?" I shook my head, pain and overwhelm making my thoughts sluggish. "What's going on?"

"The key was just left on the portal." Bella didn't turn away, her pregnant silhouette seeming to glow.

"Key? What key?"

She turned to face me. In her eyes, I saw my reflection. The single word she spoke chilled me to the bone.

"Blood."

CHAPTER 8
BELLA

W e still had time. The seals on the portal were compromised, but the leafy covering had kept most of the blood from dripping directly onto the stone and cracking it apart like an eggshell. The problem was I didn't have enough power to cover the entire thing alone.

I didn't have to, either.

Something had changed in my sister since she'd left that morning I could feel her power. It stretched like a lazy cat waking up from a nap in the sun, claws extended. She must have used her gift, though she was still playing pretend.

Donna looked up at me, her expression blank. I could see all the token protests forming. "We don't have time," I snapped. "Unless you want to see this entire town destroyed, you'll give me your hand."

I thrust my palm down in demand.

She swallowed and then leaned up. My fingers curled around hers. *Connection.*

Magic flowed between us and I pulled ruthlessly. My free hand stretched out and I called a geyser of witch's soul fire. It sprang from my fingers, brilliant blue death for anything in its path.

The bleeding man who hosted the wraith didn't have time to scream before his body was incinerated. With it all the dried leaves and moss that held his blood.

I felt Donna jerk as though trying to pull back but I tightened my grip on her. We had to get it all. Even the smallest drop would open the portal.

When the fire finally kissed nothing but stone, I released it. The quaking had stopped. Anything other than the magical protections on the portal would have been incinerated. Soul fire burned faster and hotter than regular flames, the blue light more intense than the core of a star. Channeling it took tremendous power. Even with Donna on the magical assist, I felt exhausted and weak in the knees.

"You... you killed him." Donna stared at the spot where the wraith-ridden man had been.

"He left me no choice." If I hadn't cauterized his wounds, more blood could have dripped onto the portal. The wraith had been freed and was off doing whatever the hell the things did to seek out new hosts.

That had been too close.

Axel approached. His arms were full of frightened werewolf. He set Joseline on her four feet and came over to steady me. "You okay, Bells? Need to sit down?"

"I'm fine," I said. "But my sister is hurt. Take her up to the house. I'll call for a healer."

"What about little miss?" He gestured toward the small werewolf.

Joseline had sidled up beside Donna and pressed herself into my sister's side. Kendra had stayed in human form so she could translate between us and the were-wolves. She approached and studied the young girl with her head cocked in a very canine sort of way.

"She says Donna smells safe. She wants to stay with her."

"Is that all right?" I asked my shell-shocked sister.

Joseline whined and butted her head up under Donna's hand.

"Fine," she whispered.

I exchanged a look with Axel who nodded.

"Come on, Don. You're with me." Careful of her injured ankle, he scooped her up off the ground and held her to his chest. Donna's arms went around him, more out of startled reflex. The werewolf trailed them back to his truck. After settling Donna in the cab, he lowered the tailgate for the werewolf.

I watched as they disappeared over the rise, heading toward the house.

Kendra asked, "Do you want me to set up a guard around the portal?"

I wanted to say that my wards would be enough. The werewolves weren't my employees, they were my guests. But we had barely skirted disaster. If Donna hadn't been brimming with spell craft, if I had been moments later, if the portal hadn't been covered by leaves and moss, we would be staring into the maw of the abyss.

"I would appreciate it," I said to Kendra.

"We'll pair up in twos. Do four-hour rotations so everyone stays sharp." She hesitated. "I'm not sure Joseline will want to come back to the bunkhouse. She never settled in well there and after the attack...." She trailed off.

"Did you find out anything about our other guest?"

She nodded. "Registered sex offender in Tampa. Out on parole."

I felt sick as I stared at the ashes still fluttering down to the ground. "They were working together."

Kendra sighed. "One to act as a distraction and one to head for the portal to make the blood sacrifice."

Cooperation was new behavior from the wraiths. Were they getting smarter? Or did it have something to do with the creature who called himself Declan?

Only one way to find out.

Donna's keys were lying on the ground next to her cell phone. I bent and felt a small fluttering in my midsection. I straightened and, out of instinct, wrapped my arm around my belly.

"Don't worry, little ones. He can't have you. No matter what."

I'd let the world burn first.

Donna

SHOCK. I was in shock. That was the only thing that explained why I was shivering even though the temperature was close to ninety. I sat in Axel's truck once more, staring at my trembling hands.

Bella had just...killed someone. Right in front of me.

And I'd helped her do it.

"Don, talk to me." Axel's low easy voice tugged me from my whirling thoughts.

"What are you?" I asked.

His hands clenched into fists on the wheel. "I don't know. I'm a foundling, remember?"

"The way you moved back there. I've never seen anything like it." So fast, too fast to track with the naked eye. Had he broken the sound barrier? I hadn't heard a sonic boom, but I'd been distracted what with the earthquake and all.

"It's just something I've always been able to do." He sounded uncomfortable like he didn't want to discuss it further.

"Like Bella," I shivered again, the motion causing pain to rip along my nerve endings.

"No, not like Bella. Or you. I've never seen anything like that."

"I didn't do anything." The words were automatic.

He glanced at me before refocusing on the road.

"I never had gifts," I said. "Never could work even the simplest spell. As a legacy witch, I was a disappointment, especially with Bella setting the gold standard."

"Did you ever think maybe you gave up too soon?" Axel asked. "That maybe you weren't supposed to come into your powers until later?"

"That's not the way legacies work," I corrected.

He shrugged. "All I know is that I've always been different. And that set me apart."

"Me too." I winced when he hit a particularly rough pothole.

"Sorry." He said nothing else, for which I was grateful. My mind was far too cluttered to grasp a single thread of understanding.

We pulled up in front of the house where Hyde and Clyde stood guard. Axel lowered the tailgate and the werewolf lept down and followed him to the passenger's side of the truck.

"Hang on, hot stuff," he said and then scooped me into his arms as though I weighed no more than a feather pillow.

My arms went around his neck and I absorbed the warmth he unwittingly offered. I didn't want to go back into the manor but thought I could handle it if Axel stayed with me.

"Upstairs or down?" he asked.

I couldn't stomach the thought of that too-cluttered bedroom. "Down. Easier for the healer when she gets here."

Healers, or white light energy workers, were the rarest cast of witches. The neighboring coven had one though and she was old as the hills. Matilda Longshanks had treated us for everything from chicken pox to scuffed knees when we'd been children. She also took her payment in alcohol so it was a damn good thing Bella had a bartender on her payroll.

Axel set me down on the chaise and the wolf padded in to sit next to me. When I'd first seen her in the woods

I'd thought she was huge. But after seeing her next to the other wolves, I knew she was only half their size. Her coat was pure white and a little bit matted where blood had dried on the soft fur.

"You need a bath," I said to her.

Axel raised a brow. "You're going to bathe a werewolf?"

"Why not?" I was hoping if I treated her more like a girl and less like a beast, Joseline would decide it was safe to come back to the surface. "Besides, there's no way she's sleeping in bed with me as she is."

Joseline inched a little bit closer.

A loud pounding sounded on the front door.

"That will be the healer." Axel left to go let her in.

"You be nice," I told Joseline. "No biting anyone in the house, you hear?"

She woofed slightly which I took for an agreement.

"Now, where's the patient?" Matilda Longshanks had a very heavy Yankee accent. She was brisk and to the point and seeing her apple cheeks and cherry red curls along with snapping blue eyes brought a smile to my face.

"Well, Donna Sanders, there you sit in all your glory. Been a dog's age since I've seen this one." She marched in and set down her basket full of herbs. She wore a long red dress covered by a stained apron. The pockets bulged. We must have caught her in the middle of foraging.

Axel hovered in the doorway. "Can I get you anything—?"

"Away with you." Matilda dismissed him with a wave.

Still, he hovered, looking at me as though waiting for confirmation that I didn't want him to stay.

"Thank you for everything," I said.

He licked his lips, nodded once, and then left.

"Quite the conquest you made there, missy." Matilda chuckled as she settled herself on a footstool.

"It's not like——," my words broke off in a hiss of pain when she touched my injured ankle.

White light emanated from her hands. "That's the spot, all right. Broke it completely. I'll be able to patch this up in no time. Go easy for a day or two and make sure to drink plenty of rum."

"Isn't it supposed to be water?" I hissed as her hands glided lightly over me.

"Now where's the fun in that? How's that boy of yours? What was his name? Derick?"

"Devon." I knew what she was doing, asking me questions to take my mind off the pain. It wasn't working but I answered anyway. "He's good. Just started college. Ouch!"

Joseline growled.

"Had to be set so she doesn't end up with one leg longer than the other." I wasn't sure if Matilda was talking to me or the wolf. And I didn't care. After the last flash of pain, I was starting to relax.

Healing via energy manipulation required massive amounts of energy from both the healer and the person being healed. A broken ankle might require a nap. Anything more serious would result in both parties being bedridden for days to recover.

The pain faded from the blazing agony to a dull throbbing. I sagged in relief.

"Well, I think that will do," Matilda let out a jaw-cracking yawn. "I better head home for a nap while I still can."

"You can stay here." It was an offer made out of habit.

"You know I can't. Good seeing you, Donna. I'll just leave my invoice with pretty boy."

Witches from other covens wouldn't let their guard down in a rival family's territory. While we might be on decent terms and willing to share skills, we weren't friends. I listened to her heavy footsteps as she retreated from the room. I shivered and a moment later, felt the warm press of fur as Joseline climbed up beside me.

"You shouldn't be on the furniture like that," I said groggily.

She snuffled but made no move to get down.

More footsteps. The sound of the door closing once more. "Don?"

"Tired," I murmured.

"Get some sleep." Maybe it was my imagination but I thought I felt his hand in my hair as I drifted off.

Bella

THE DEVILLE FISHTAILED as I sped up the set of gravel-covered switchbacks that led to the hotel Declan had purchased. At least I was pretty sure I was on the right road. Unfortunately, there was no huge flashing sign, *the demon is this way.* My palms began to sweat and my nervous system moved to DEFCON 2.

I felt it the moment I crossed over his wards. Like a hundred invisible spiders crawling over my flesh. The unnerving sensation was meant to make a witch hesitate, to think twice before crossing into the demon's territory.

But Declan had breeched my wards first. And I couldn't ignore the demon any longer. No matter how much I wanted to.

The hotel was a relic, or it had been the last time I'd come up this way. Overgrown, with Virginia creeper and ivy entombing the structure to the point where it was impossible to tell at a glance what sort of building material had been used in its construction. The river had been damned up to form a lake that was surrounded by evergreens and rhododendrons and smelled like a bog. The clay on the tennis courts had been riddled with cracks. Weeds had grown over the long drive. Once it had been a rich man's weekend home, a place where he and his family could "enjoy nature" while still maintaining their lavish lifestyle. Too lavish as the family had lost their money during the last recession and no one had been able to afford to buy the neglected property.

Until I'd summoned a demon.

The gravel was fresh and thick, the bushes trimmed, and the lake clean of the stagnant

gray-green swamp water. New clay had been poured on the tennis court, the old net replaced with a new one, and the lines freshly painted. The court looked ready for a game. The grounds were neat and inviting, the perfect lure. White iron benches sat beneath shady oaks and maples and a white stone path led down to the lake.

I had no idea where Declan got his money but he seemed to conjure it out of thin air. This

was the first property of three the demon had purchased, the only one that was open to guests. His home base. I'd spent many a sleepless night trying to determine what exactly his endgame was and how I could stop him.

He met me on the steps just as I'd put the DeVille in park. The demon was in his mortal guise, the skin fitting him as well as his expensive black suit. The top two buttons of his dress shirt were unfastened and he held a highball glass with two fingers of amber liquid. He appeared every inch the wealthy hotel mogul kicking back at the end of the day.

"Bella," he murmured. "Miss me already?"

I maneuvered my pregnant bulk out from behind the wheel and called magic as I turned to face him. It glowed like bioluminescent organisms as it floated in my hands. "Your plan didn't work, *Declan.*"

He cocked his head to one side, his expression giving nothing away. "And what plan would that be, witchling?"

"The one where one of your wraiths distracts my people and leaves the portal free to be opened." A psychic wind from the soul plane blew my hair back from my face. I was sure the demon could see his reflection in my mirrored eyes. "They attacked a *child*, you bastard."

"Put your claws away, kitten, before you scare off all the paying customers." Declan moved closer and lowered his voice. "And what makes you so sure that they are my wraiths?"

Quick as a striking snake, he ensnared my left wrist. I felt the magic sputter and die, like an engine that refused to turn over. My entire body felt frozen. I hadn't known he could drain me like that.

Still, it wasn't in me to show weakness, even when I was at a disadvantage. "Are you saying they aren't your wraiths?"

"That's precisely what I'm saying." The demon nodded to an elderly couple that was coming up the steps. "Come, walk with me."

Before I could protest, the demon adjusted his hold so that one arm was around what, once upon a time, had been my waist. He ushered me over to the gravel path, away from the mortals.

"Amazingly, you are still alive," Declan murmured once we were out of earshot of anyone else. "Haven't you read the histories about what happens to witches who show their powers to mortals?"

"Humanity has come a long way since the witch trials." I shook my head and then scowled at him. "And don't change the subject. I want to know how you got the wraiths to work together."

Declan stopped walking and turned to face me, withdrawing his hand and with it, the choke chain on my magic. "I already told you, witchling. They aren't my wraiths."

"Why should I believe you?" My chin went up at a defiant angle.

"Because I already have what I want. What every demon wants. I have been summoned. And because you refuse to sign the contract, I am free to build a life on this plane. Opening the portal does nothing to improve my situation, witchling."

"Quit calling me that," I snapped.

"Apologies, poppet." He winked at me.

I huffed out a breath. I wanted to rail at him, but not about the nicknames. "So you really didn't call the wraiths?"

"I really didn't," he agreed.

A sinking feeling took root in my stomach. I believed the demon. Maybe it was foolish, he was a demon, one of the banished magical practitioners too powerful to be allowed in the mortal realm. But he seemed...proud of the life he'd been building over the past several months.

"If you didn't summon the wraiths," I asked. "Then who did?"

"I don't know." He reached out and tucked a stray lock of hair behind my ear. "But I think we need to find out."

"We?" I raised a brow even as excitement filled my chest. "You'll let me study the demon archives?"

"For endless hours if you so desire, witchling." His lips curled up at the edges. "For a price."

"What price?"

He tapped his lips as though thinking it through. "A kiss."

I leaned forward, intending to lay one on him real quick so I could get to the archives but he pulled back.

"Not now. At the time of my choosing."

"Fine then," I said. "It's a bargain."

"A bargain well struck," the demon said and then gestured toward the steps. "Ladies first."

CHAPTER 9
DONNA

The same dream again. The big house, the finished upstairs floor, the sea of extra rooms on the lower level. Overwhelm setting in. It wasn't even my stuff and I was drowning in the endless expanse of it.

But then the dream changed. The hoard was pushed back and I spied a path. I followed it, snaking around the useless debris until I came to the prettiest space of all. A corner room with plenty of natural light and a fireplace. Once I cleared the clutter, it would make a perfect sanctuary. The place I'd been looking for. There was a door leading to the outside world. Eager to explore the garden I moved to it, only to find it yanked open.

Strangers walking in. They were using my space without my permission, invading my territory. I needed to get a lock, a deadbolt, I had to keep them out. But they just kept coming and coming....

I sat up, heart pounding, and swung my feet over the side of the bed.

And stepped on something furry. It yelped and I snatched my feet back up.

"What the shit?" I asked just as the door burst open.

"Don?" Axel stood there, an anxious look on his face. "Is everything all right?"

My heart was pounding and my mouth felt mossy because I'd been in such a deep sleep. I still wore the dress I'd borrowed from Bella and I could tell that my hair was flattened on one side and stuck out sideways on the other.

Not exactly at my best for facing the perfection that was Axel.

"Is it your ankle?" He moved to the side of the bed, his dark blond brows pulled tightly together.

"What? No. That's fine. I stepped on something."

"Joseline?" Axel asked.

A canine nose appeared over the other side.

"What's she doing down there?" My heart was still hammering, both from fright and embarrassment.

"She hasn't left your side," Axel said. "You said you didn't want her in bed with you until she bathed. Considering what happened, I didn't think she'd want me to do it,"

In answer, Joseline bared her teeth.

"No," I told her sternly. "Axel is a friend. We don't threaten our friends."

The snarl died and she whined softly.

"Has she changed back?" I asked Axel.

He shook his head. "I'm not sure that she can."

Sometimes werewolves who'd endured trauma couldn't regain their human form. It made sense. A wolf, even a small wolf, had an easier time protecting itself than a young girl. The danger was that the longer Joseline clung to the wolf's shape, the more likely it was that she would lose her identity and eventually, her knowledge of even being human.

"Maybe you ought to give us a minute," I said to Axel.

He met my gaze and then nodded in understanding. I called his name when he reached the door though and he turned back.

"Thank you."

He bowed his head in acknowledgment. "Anytime, Don. All you have to do is ask."

He shut the door, leaving me alone with the werewolf.

Careful to move slowly, I got up and headed toward the cluttered desk. A candle stood there, a cream pillar that smelled of gardenias. It sat on a crystal plate alongside a matchbox. I picked up the matches and struck one. Bella could light a candle with the snap of her fingers since she was six, but as the dud, I'd need the means. The match tip flared to life in a tiny orange and yellow blaze. I touched it against the untried wick waiting until the cotton caught before blowing the match out. Candle in hand, I headed around the foot of the bed to where Joseline had backed herself into the corner between my bed and the heavy drapes that covered the window.

Though my back would probably make me pay for it later, I lowered myself to the floor in front of her, careful not to meet her gaze or do anything the wolf would perceive as a challenge.

"When I was little, I had awful nightmares. I'd wake

up screaming almost every night. My Grand taught me a trick that has helped. Whenever your mind starts spinning with bad thoughts and memories, especially in the dark, you light a candle and stare at the flame. Watch it closely. Sometimes it will flicker, other times it will be completely still. Whatever else it does, it chases the shadows away."

I didn't say anything else, just sat there and watched the flame myself, giving her privacy to work through whatever she needed to work through while remaining close so she wasn't alone.

Heartbeat. Heartbeat. Heartbeat. The scent of gardenias filled the space between us. The flame swayed, pulled by an air current as a light summer breeze caressed the house. I'd forgotten exactly how soothing the little mindfulness exercise could be and lost myself to it. The terror of the dream, of my perfect space being invaded, began to ebb until I was left with only a sense of peace.

When I finally looked up a little girl with curly dark hair and solemn brown eyes stared at me. She was naked. Her skin was crusted with dirt and blood. I could count her ribs beneath her warm brown skin. She looked ready to bolt at the slightest movement on my part.

"Hey you," I said and smiled at her.

She scrambled up and before I understood her intention, she crossed the distance and flung herself against me. As though she needed someone to hold her together, while she fell apart.

I could relate.

"It's all right now," I told Joseline as she sobbed

silently against me. "You're safe here with me. I promise."

FRESH FROM THE SHOWER, I was clad once again in a bathrobe, my hair wrapped up in a towel. I'd wanted Joseline to go first, but she'd backed herself into a corner, so I'd stripped off the ruined dress and washed my hair and body thoroughly.

Clean, I waited on the other side of the cracked bathroom door while the water ran in the shower. She hadn't spoken a word yet, but I did hear the steady spray interrupted so figured she must have gotten into the tub.

The sounds of footsteps made me turn. Axel stood there, a plastic shopping bag in one hand. "I went to the bunkhouse earlier. Picked up Joseline's things."

I took the small bag that contained nothing but a nightgown, two pairs of sweats, and two short sleeve shirts. No shoes, no coat, no books, or stuffed animals for comfort. A pink toothbrush sat on top. All the girl's possessions in the world.

I huffed out a breath. "Thank you."

Axel touched my hand lightly. "You can get her more."

I nodded and forced a smile. "The two of us can go shopping together." If she could handle the bright lights and people-filled spaces.

"Have you given up hope on getting back into your house?" he asked.

The house. Mental forehead smack. "I forgot. Where's Bella?"

Axel frowned. "She hasn't come back yet."

I scrubbed a hand over my face. "I need her to lift the curse she put on my husband."

A low growling sound filled the space. My gaze went to the bathroom door, thinking it was Joseline before I noticed that Axel had balled his hands into fists.

"It's you?" I asked him, stunned.

His eyes slid shut and he drew in a deep breath. "Sorry. I don't like thinking about your husband."

"That makes two of us." I breathed and moved closer to him. "Axel...what are you?"

He shook his head. "I don't know."

"Can you shift?" I asked.

He shook his head. "No. I'm not a shifter. Not a witch or a goblin or demon or fae, or anything else that Bella knows about either."

That covered all the possibilities.

"Even among the monsters, there's no one like me." Gone was his easygoing manner and his eyes looked bleak as they fixed on my face. "I'm a freak, Don."

I recalled the way he'd lept into the fight earlier with no regard for his safety. He said he didn't shift and couldn't work magic.

"You're not a freak," I said to him. "You're unique."

He laughed, but there was no humor in it.

I put my right hand over one of his clenched fists and tried to ignore the spark I felt from touching his skin. "It's all right. Whatever you are, it's better than being a dud in this world."

"You're not a dud, Don." Stormy gray eyes studied my face. "I feel magic every time I look at you."

"That isn't possible." I was just plain old magically ungifted Donna. The neurotic sister. The resource suck that wasn't worth training.

His gray eyes were intense as they searched my face. "You aren't a dud," he repeated.

My lip curled up. "Do you think you can convince me out of something I've known my entire life?"

"Isn't that what you want me to do?"

I swallowed and tried to pull my hand away from him. He caught it in his other one, not allowing me to retreat. "How about a deal? I'll try to believe what you're saying if you do the same for me."

"I don't even want magic." I swallowed as I admitted my deepest-held secret. "It's cost me too much already."

"Did you ever think that's why you haven't been able to access your gifts? You've rejected your legacy," he murmured. "Maybe it can give you something back if you let it in."

My lips parted. I wanted to tell him it was impossible. No amount of playing make-believe would change the truth of my situation.

He took a step closer to me until every breath I took was filled with his fresh air and spring rain scent. "So, do we have a deal?"

Try he said. That wasn't a big ask. I could try. Putting in the effort was something I knew. Hard work. Struggle. Perseverance. Sweat equity I could manage.

"And you'll try, too?" I asked.

When he nodded, I held out my hand. "Agreed."

He lifted my hand to his lips and brushed a soft kiss over the knuckles. "It's a bargain well struck."

Those words... The sort the fae used to seal a deal. But Axel wasn't fae. He didn't have the jewel-toned irises. And much like demons, fae couldn't remain in the mortal world for long.

The water shut off in the bathroom. Axel squeezed my hand once more and then let go. "Come down when you're ready. I'm making homemade pizza."

I watched him walk away and tried to ignore all the inappropriate feelings that my sister's PA stirred in me. He was too young for me. I was too old for him. He didn't know what he was.

He was also incredibly kind. And the way he looked at me, the intensity of his gaze. stirred embers that had been banked for a long time.

But I was married. And while that might not mean anything to Lewis Allen, it had meant something to me.

Lewis. Frick, I kept forgetting about him. After checking on Joseline I headed into the bedroom and plucked up my cell. I called Bella's number but it rang through to voicemail.

"Meet me at my house," I said and then turned to go.

And let out a breathless shriek when Annabeth appeared right in front of me.

"I know where she is," the poltergeist cast me a coy look. "I can go to her if you pay the toll."

The toll, aka the blood toll. Three drops of my blood were freely offered so Annabeth could become corporeal for a short while. I knew better than to bargain with the spirit. "Pass," I said and walked around her intending to leave.

"Don't you even want to know who the father of her children is?"

I hesitated. "Bella will tell me if she wants me to know."

I felt the air grow colder as Annabeth glided closer to me. "And the other one? The pretty boy? I can find out what he is."

Too much temptation there. But if Axel had wanted to know, he would have already made the bargain with the Southern Belle. She was just looking to double down. "Piss off, Annabeth. I'm not interested in making deals with you."

I headed to the bathroom once more but Annabeth called out, "He's right you know. You aren't a dud, just a very *very* late bloomer."

"What?" I whirled around but she had already faded from view, even as her disembodied laughter echoed through the hallway.

My heart was hammering hard against my ribcage. This house and its inhabitants...no wonder my sister was nuts.

The bathroom door opened. Joseline stood there wearing her sweats and a t-shirt. Her hair needed oiling and wrapping, which I could do for her after she ate.

And after I dealt with Lewis.

"You hungry?" I asked and she nodded almost eagerly.

"Awesome." I linked my arm with hers and we headed downstairs to help with the pizza making.

CHAPTER 10

DONNA

T he pizza was excellent. Better than any takeout in town, which I told Axel.

He grinned. "It's all in the water."

Joseline reached for another slice, her fifth.

"What do you think?" I asked the werewolf. "Best pizza in town, yeah?"

She met my gaze and nodded but didn't utter a word.

"Help me clean up, Don." Axel gestured for me to come into the kitchen. When I

followed he lowered his voice. "The others said she doesn't talk. At all. Hasn't spoken a word since she showed up at the bunk house."

I blew out a sigh and cut my gaze toward the dining room door. "Emotional trauma? Or is it physical do you think?"

He shook his head. "There's no way to tell without her medical records."

"Which the werewolves never show up with." I sighed.

He put a hand on my arm. "You got her to change back. She trusts us enough to eat

and get cleaned up. That's much better than she was a few hours ago."

I wrapped my arms around myself as Axel started loading the dishwasher. "I know. I just wish I could do more to help her. She doesn't deserve this."

Axel nodded but didn't say anything else.

"Can you give me a ride back to my car?" I asked him, changing the subject. It was about two miles over unpaved roads to the portal and though my leg was healed, I didn't want to risk another mishap.

He frowned. "You're going out tonight?"

"There's something I have to try and fix."

He shut the dishwasher and then straightened up. "I'll go with you."

"You don't have to."

"I want to."

I opened my mouth ready to argue with him when Joseline came into the kitchen and slipped her hand into mine.

So it was the three of us crammed into Axel's truck that headed into Shadow Cove. The second we turned onto my street I spotted the gathered crowd on my front lawn.

Lewis was exactly where I'd left him, a foot away from the open front door. No one stood closer than three feet. I saw Mindy at the front, her face beautifully tearstained in the moonlight.

Axel parked across the street. Joseline had shifted

back into her werewolf form. I wasn't sure if it was for her protection or mine.

I bit my thumbnail, a bad habit that I indulged in whenever I was mega-stressed. I didn't want to get out of the car and have all those gazes swing my way. I didn't want to hear the whispers that I was just like my crazy sister.

Axel turned to face me. "Do you want us to come with you?"

I did. And I thought that maybe that was exactly why I should do this on my own. "No, thanks. I'm not sure I can do much of anything anyway."

He leaned back into the seat, casually slinging his arm over the seat back. "Remember our bargain, Don. I'll try to believe if you do."

I nodded and then gestured for Joseline to climb over me so I could exit the truck. She did so, reluctantly.

The crowd hushed as I approached the spot where Lewis stood, still enclosed in the invisible box. Mindy eyed me warily.

Try to believe that I wasn't a dud. That somehow, in some weird way, I had gathered magic and done this to my husband.

I was a legacy witch. A Sanders of Shadow Cove.

"Please," Lewis croaked. His dishwater brown hair was plastered to his forehead and his skin sagged like a Basset Hound. "Please, Donna. I'm sorry. I'll give you whatever you want if you just let me out."

I opened my mouth, ready to tell him that I hadn't done anything when I heard Axel's voice in my head. *I'll try to believe if you do.*

The problem was, I didn't believe I had magic any more than I believed the sun would rise in the west tomorrow. But maybe I could fake it.

And Lewis had said anything.

"I want the house," I said in a rush and then held my breath.

"No," Mindy cried but Lewis was nodding. "Of course. I'll have my lawyer add it to the divorce settlement."

I stared at him for a long minute. He'd agreed just like that? After changing the locks and moving his tart into my home?

And more than that I realized that Lewis was still hell-bent on divorcing me. And that...hurt. Not because he didn't want me but because now that Devon was gone, it was clear that he didn't value me. At all. Was ready to wash his hands of me.

Had he ever loved me? Or had I just been conveniently biddable because I would have done anything to be something other than Donna Sanders, the dud witch? Bella's lesser sister.

As though summoned by my thoughts, the crowd parted and Bella glided forward. She looked particularly witchy in tall high-heeled boots. Her thin black dress clung to the mound of her pregnancy. I thought I heard more than one person murmur, the words "Devil's spawn."

Bella raised an eyebrow as she studied the man in the invisible box then turned her back on him.

"Go get whatever you need from the house, sister."

Her voice had an eerie quality, like wind blowing through an underground cavern.

"No," Mindy cried out, moving to intercept me as I headed to the house. But Bella reached out and gripped the young woman by the arm. Her eyes were mirrors when Mindy looked at her.

"I see you," Bella whispered in her witchy voice. "I see that you want to take what isn't yours. What you haven't earned."

Oh shit. Bella was holding her spiritual mirror up so that Mindy could take a good long look at her choices. And airing her dirty laundry in front of the neighborhood. If it had been anybody else, I might have intervened. As it was, I hurried up the steps and through the unlocked door, desperate to pack and get my sister out of there as soon as possible.

I beelined for my bedroom and went straight to the closet. I pulled down a suitcase that hit the bamboo floor with a thump. I packed jeans and sneakers, t-shirts, shorts, and sweaters. Pajamas, bras, socks, and underwear. A pair of heavy boots and my rain jacket. My heavy winter coat wouldn't fit so I put it on. After scooping up my jewelry box and phone charger, I headed into the bathroom. In a plastic bag, I bundled up shampoo, conditioner, body wash and facial cleaners, Hand lotion, face cream, makeup brushes, hairbrush, comb, deodorant, and makeup all went into a traveling case.

Two minutes later I barreled down the stairs, dragging the suitcase and travel case in my wake. No time for anything else. I had to get Bella out of here.

Mindy was in a ball on the ground, rocking back and

forth as Bella looked on with dispassionate mirrored eyes.

Lewis trembled inside his invisible prison.

"Enough," I said, and I meant it. Bella looked up and a moment later, Lewis fell forward, practically belly-flopping on top of Mindy.

The neighbors made a hole and I ushered my sister toward her car, not saying a word.

"You did that," she breathed. "You worked that spell."

"I'll see you at home," I told her and then winced when I realized what I'd just said. "I mean the manor."

Bella's eyes had returned to normal and maybe it was my imagination but she looked sad.

"See you soon," she said and slammed the car door.

Axel was out of the truck, his gray eyes glinting with amusement as he took my traveling case and suitcase and stowed them in the bed of the pick-up.

The neighbors goggled at the two of us.

"We'll be the talk of the town by lunch tomorrow," I said to him.

He winked at me, playful Axel back at the helm. "Then let's give them something to talk about."

And he kissed me.

He was warm and hard and tasted a little bit tangy, like pizza sauce. He smelled of ozone, like the clean air after a storm. He filled my senses and shorted out my wonky brain until I forgot about it, and everything that wasn't Axel. No matter what he said, it wasn't a kiss for anyone else's benefit. It was an *I'm heading off to war and this might be the last time I get to do this* sort of kiss. Full of desperation and longing and a desire so potent it made my head swim.

And then it was over. He stepped back, gray eyes wary. I wondered if he thought I was going to smack him. I wondered if maybe I should.

But I smiled, a funny lopsided sort of grin. "Come on, let's go home," I breathed.

He grinned back and opened the passenger's side door. Joseline hopped down and I slid back into the middle seat. And then gave the goggling neighbors the finger.

Yesterday, they'd watched me hauled off in the back of a police vehicle. After years of being the neighbor who would drop everything to help them whenever there was a need. Some of them must have seen what Lewis had been up to but no one had called to warn me.

So fuck them.

I had a more pressing concern.

"You let him out?" Axel said.

I'd felt it. Like a thread snapping when I'd spoken the word, enough. Whatever that spell had been, I was the one who'd stopped it.

I swallowed past the lump in my throat. "Yeah, I guess I did."

He closed his hand over mine. It was warm and calloused and while it was inappropriate as hell, I was too elated to care.

Maybe I wasn't a dud after all.

But then another thought occurred. What exactly was my power?

THE DEVILLE WAS PARKED in front of the steps when we returned to the house. That didn't mean my sister was inside. She could be anywhere on the grounds. I had something I needed to do before I went hunting for her.

Joseline had shifted back to human and wore her sweats and a bright blue t-shirt. I'd draped a towel over her shoulders to protect the garment. She sat at the kitchen table, swinging her legs, and watched as I rummaged through the cabinets.

Axel stood against the counter and watched. "If you'd tell me what you were looking for—"

"Found it." I emerged with a bottle of avocado oil.

When he raised a brow I said, "My college roommate had textured curls like Joseline. If the hair isn't oiled properly, it's prone to frizz and breakage. She used to have me do this every night for her. We used the kitchen oil as it's more economical than the salon crap that's infused with a bunch of stuff that doesn't make a difference. And in return, she helped me through chemistry. We made our own infusions a couple of times with rose-hips and lavender."

Axel watched as I poured the avocado oil onto my palms and rubbed them together before I began working on the little girl's head. I could see her reflection in the refrigerator. Her eyes were shut and she leaned back into me as I worked my way slowly through the mass of kinks and knots.

By the time I could get my fingers through her hair, her head was beginning to nod. After washing my hands,

I rummaged in my bag until I found the scarf I'd packed for exactly this purpose. I wrapped it around Joseline's hair so that the moisture would seep in while she slept.

"Would it be okay if Axel brought you upstairs?" I asked Joseline. "I need to talk to my sister but I'll be up soon."

If she said no, I'd go with her and stay with her.

But she must have begun to trust Axel because she slid off the stool and let him lead her to the staircase.

I found Bella in our mother's old bedroom. She was hunting through a giant wooden box and muttering to herself. The place was a certified disaster, clothes and papers and items for spells strewn everywhere.

"What are you doing?" I asked her.

She whirled to face me, a hand going to her throat. "You scared me."

She looked lost. And maybe even afraid.

"Sit down before you fall down," I instructed.

She sank into a nearby armchair. Her eyes were rimmed with red.

"You okay?" I asked. "We can call the healer back if you need—"

"I'm fine." She said quickly. "Just stressed."

I wanted to ask her about what had happened at my house. About the thread. I'd tugged it loose with one word. *Enough*. But she didn't look like she could handle questions right now.

She looked like someone being crushed under the weight of secrets.

"Bells?" I asked as I approached the chair.

She didn't jerk or startle when I called her name. She didn't appear to have heard me at all.

I knelt before her, trying not to grimace as my knees hit the too-thin rug. "Hey, talk to me, sis. I'm worried about you."

"I'm worried about all of us," she murmured and then slowly, turned her head to face me. Took in what I was wearing.

"I hope it's okay that I borrowed this," I said when she didn't speak.

Her eyes met mine. "I bought it for you."

"What?" I frowned.

"It's become a habit of mine. I see something that I think you'd like and get it. I buy things for you all the time. Things I think you would like or would look good in. You have terrible taste."

My jaw dropped. "I do not."

"Do too." The ghost of a smile graced her lips. "At least when it comes to clothes. And husbands."

I opened my mouth, ready to retort when I realized I had nothing to say.

"Was he really preferable to us?" Bella asked.

"That's not an easy question." I swallowed. "I hated being here, being reminded of what I was lacking."

She put her hand over mine. "You felt it tonight, didn't you?"

I swallowed and nodded.

"Tell me what happened earlier. Talk it through. Maybe it will spark some sort of memory."

My lids lowered and I curled my fingers around the

arm of the chair, gripping it tight to hold me in place even as I traveled back in my mind to that morning.

"Axel dropped me off. Lewis met me out front. I realized Mindy was still there. He'd essentially moved her in."

"How did you feel?" Bella asked carefully.

I knew why she was asking. Soul magic was often triggered by strong emotions. Anger, desire, and fear had all been known to jumpstart a witch's powers.

But I'd felt all those things many times over the years, there was nothing new here, nothing I hadn't felt before except....

"Betrayed," I said. "Not because he was cheating. But because everything he said and did was designed to hurt me. I'd trusted him and he weaponized that trust and used it against me."

As I spoke the words, I knew them to be true. Lewis picked a younger woman to have an affair with, underscoring all the insecurities I'd been struggling with regarding aging. He'd moved her into the home I loved. Another betrayal. And the nail in the coffin was when he said I was just like Bella. When he'd called me a freak.

I swallowed and opened my eyes, fixed my gaze on my sister.

"He wouldn't let me be me," I murmured. "I was trapped in a lie."

"So you trapped him in turn," Bella said softly. "Comeuppance."

"What?" I squeezed the hand I held.

"That's your power, Donna. An eye for an eye. He

hurt you and contained you and you did the same to him."

My mouth fell open. No, it couldn't be possible.

But there had been that tearing sensation, as though something inside me was breaking loose. And it had felt...right.

"Comeuppance," I breathed.

"Took you long enough, you stubborn witch." Her gaze drifted back to the cold hearth.

I swallowed. "Is this about the portal?"

"Yes, and no." She licked her lips. "Do you believe in it now?"

"After feeling the ground shake, it's hard not to." I still hadn't allowed myself to think about how Bella had incinerated that man earlier. It was too much to process on top of everything else.

I focused on her instead. "Bella, talk to me. Tell me what's going on."

She shook her head.

Her hands were cold and bloodlessly pale. "Hey, I know I've been difficult about things in the past. But I'm here now and I want to help. Talk to me."

Slowly, so slowly, she drew her hands and my hands on top of them to the mounded bump of her belly. "I summoned a demon."

CHAPTER 11

BELLA

Another sleepless night. The pregnancy bulk made me uncomfortable. I lay on my back and my insides felt like they were being crushed. I turned on my side and my back hurt. When I finally did get comfortable, I had to get up to pee. Worst of all, I couldn't forget the look on Donna's face when I confessed what I'd done.

I'd been so close to getting her back. Donna had embraced her powers in front of half the town. She wasn't living in denial anymore, clinging to her home-organizing business like she didn't have a greater destiny waiting for her to walk the path. It was what I'd wanted, to get my sister back.

So why did it feel like she was slipping away again?

Restless, I walked the length of the corridors. Anna-beth trailed along behind me, making offers, hoping I would take her up on a blood payment.

Like I hadn't struck enough bad deals already.

If only Donna would let me explain what had

happened. I shouldn't have led with *I summoned a demon.* It cast an ugly shadow over my character. And she already thought I was a murderer.

Maybe I was, but after hearing the background on the man I'd burned, I'd decided I could live with the death of a pedophile.

Axel met me on the stairs and handed me a steaming mug. "You okay, Bells?"

I stared down into the murky depths of the mug. "I honestly don't know."

"I think there's a lot of that going around," Axel murmured. "I'm here if you want to talk about it."

I nodded and sipped the morning brew. "Thanks. You're a good egg, Axel."

He nodded and headed into the kitchen while I went out onto the patio. The grass was kissed with early morning dew, the sun casting long shadows from the trees. My phone buzzed and I fished it out of an inner pocket, checking the incoming text from Kendra.

Kendra: Shift change. Hardee har har.
*Bella: *eye roll* Any signs of wraiths?*
Kendra: Nothing. How's J?
Bella: My sister convinced her to shift for dinner last night.
Kendra: Good 2 hear. Keep me posted
Bella: You too.

How long could I keep this up? The werewolves weren't my employees. They had enough to deal with. I believed Declan when the demon said he wasn't behind the attacks.

That meant another demon was trying to open the portal.

Who would have summoned it? And where was it hiding?

Footsteps sounded behind me. I turned and spotted Donna. She wore a black suit with heels and Jackie-O sunglasses covered her eyes. A suitcase and a travel makeup kit sat by her left side while Joseline, in human form, stood to her right.

"You're leaving." It wasn't a question.

She nodded once.

Icy terror gripped me by the spine. I didn't know what to say. All the spells I knew, all the enchantments and there were no words to keep my sister close.My throat felt tight as though something had lodged in there, cutting off my ability to speak.

Finally, I croaked, "Where will you go?"

"Joseline, would you give us a minute?" Donna said to the werewolf. "See if Axel can fix you some breakfast before we head out."

The girl swallowed and nodded, before slipping her hand out of Donna's. I watched her go, glad she had bonded with my sister even as I was sorry I didn't share that same closeness.

"Bella, I'm scared for you. You're in over your head. And that girl," she nodded in the direction the werewolf had gone, "She's been through enough already."

My hands went to my belly and Donna followed the gesture with her gaze. "When you're a mother, you'll understand. It guts me to think that you're beyond help—"

I flinched.

"But in the last twenty-four hours, I've seen you kill someone. And you admitted you summoned a demon. If you were anyone else, I would have called the police."

My pride prickled and I lifted my chin. "You mean *we* killed someone. You and me. Couldn't have done it without you, sis."

She pushed her sunglasses up onto her head and then pinched the bridge of her nose. "Look, I don't want to fight with you. But my mind is made up. I can't stay here."

My laugh was hollow. "So that's it. You accept your powers and still turn your back on the legacy. On me."

"*You summoned a demon.*" She spread her hands wide. "The very creatures you've spent your life fighting to contain. I can't keep up when you're busy rewriting the rules."

"Don't talk to me about the rules," I spat at her. "You have no idea, none, what I've been going through. How the weight of this damn legacy has been crushing me flat. You got to ignore your powers, pretend you didn't have any magic, and do whatever you damn well pleased. While I've been here, doing what we were meant to do together!"

She stared at me a moment. "We're two different people, Bella."

"You think I don't know that?" I asked. "Perfect little Donna would never summon a demon. Or kill a wraith-ridden man bent on suicide. She'd find another way full of unicorns and rainbows where everyone got a star sticker at the end."

"You don't know me at all," Donna whispered.

"Same, sis. Same." I looked away before I started crying.

I heard her footsteps heading back into the house. Gritting my teeth, I stepped out onto the wet lawn, wiping away the silent tears that slid down my cheeks.

I had a portal to guard.

Donna

I FOUND Axel and Joseline in the kitchen, pouring waffle batter onto a sizzling iron. Joseline's tongue poked out the side of her mouth as she concentrated on not over-filling the grid. Axel looked up and his gray gaze flicked from my face to my suitcase and back. He didn't say anything, just tipped his head to the side and waited.

Had he known about the demon? Maybe not. Bella kept her secrets close.

"So, I wanted to say thank you for everything." I plastered a smile on my face, trying to ignore the electricity between us. "Since Joseline and I are heading out."

Axel didn't move, didn't speak, just watched me with that intense gray stare. Joseline lifted the lid and then used bamboo tongs to remove the fully cooked waffle. She brought it out into the dining room, leaving the two of us alone.

"You've been...really great." I tried again. "And I really appreciate it. Really."

Internal eye-roll. I was a grown-ass woman. Why

couldn't I get through a sentence without using the word really?

Maybe because Axel still hadn't moved, hadn't blinked, was holding me captive with that stormy stare that could be soft as morning mist or as intense as a thunderstorm over the churning sea.

There were so many layers to this man. His youth and beauty and easygoing manner hid the warrior within. And also the caretaker. And the wounded soul that called out to my own with a desperate yearning until I wanted to wrap myself around him and just hold him tight.

He made me feel too much and it was too soon. I wasn't ready.

I licked suddenly dry lips. "So, thank you again."

Time to get the hell out of there before I said or did something stupid. Well, more stupid. I picked up my bags and had taken a step into the dining room when I felt his hand on my shoulder.

"Hey, Don. Aren't you forgetting something?"

"What?" I asked trying not to melt at the flash of heat which zipped through me at his touch.

"This," he breathed and kissed me.

The bags hit the floor with a *thunk*. I got lost in Axel. The taste of coffee on his lips. The scent of ozone. The feel of him hard and unyielding against my softness. Kissing him was the single most important thing in my universe. I never wanted it to end.

He was the one who put distance between our bodies, though his hands remained on my arms. I realized I'd been clutching fistfuls of his blue t-shirt and forced my fingers to let go. Then, tried to smooth the wrinkles over his pecs while regaining my composure.

His finger curled beneath my chin and he forced my gaze up to meet his.

"This isn't over," he vowed.

My lips parted and I shook my head. "It has to be."

He just smiled and left the kitchen.

Time blindness grabbed hold of me as I stood there, my luggage at my feet. I had no plan, no idea where I ought to go or what I should do. I hadn't lied to Bella. I was worried about Joseline, especially if my sister was dabbling in demon magic. And Axel complicated the hell out of everything.

But I was leaving for good. I needed to get back to work, write the proposal for Ali Smith's job and see to the messages stacking up in my inbox. I needed to get a divorce and figure out what came next. Staying at the manor and being a full-time legacy witch wasn't something I could do.

So, I forced myself to bend down and scoop up my bags. Then head out into the dining room.

"You don't need to come with me if you don't want," I said to Joseline.

In answer, she picked up her syrup-covered plate and headed into the kitchen. I heard the sound of running water and a moment later she was back, slipping her slightly sticky hand into my free one.

"Okay then," I blew out a long breath. "We'll figure something out."

Annabeth appeared as we approached the front door. "Running away again, scaredy-witch?"

"Goodbye, Annabeth," I said politely as I stepped around her transparent form. "Always a pleasure."

"Just so you know, power calls to power," Annabeth said. "You've freed your magic but you've fastened a target on your back."

I turned to ask her what she was talking about but she vanished.

"I hate it when she does that," I muttered. "Come on. We have business to be about. No cryptic spirits allowed."

Three hours later, I'd knocked several items off of my to-do list. We'd gone to Walmart. I'd worried about sensory overload, but she'd been all right with the music and lights and the store wasn't too crowded. While Joseline was in the dressing room, trying on clothes I'd done a sweep of my email. Deleting the junk and planning to reply to the people who had reached out to me for estimates. One, a blended family with seven children had two of everything and wanted to hire me to help "put their lives in order" which grabbed me right away. I loved those kinds of projects. Loved helping set people up for their happily ever after.

The one problem though, was that I couldn't drag Joseline along with me while I worked.

The bunkhouse was always an option but it had been less than a day since she'd been attacked there. I didn't want to leave her in a place she didn't feel safe.

What she needed was to be in school. Setting up a routine that would help her fit in. We couldn't risk that. Not until she had better control of her wolf. And I figured out if she could speak.

Were there supernatural psychologists to help with these things?

After loading the Impala's trunk with all of our new purchases, I googled hotels near me.

One came up, a newly opened place that looked swanky and full of amenities including tennis courts and a well-stocked pond. A few cottages were out of sight of the main building. What grabbed me though was the acres of woodlands that surrounded the place. That was exactly what Joseline needed, should the wolf rise.

After putting the directions into my GPS, I drove us up the series of switchbacks, heading to our destination. The sun was out and Joseline was smiling as she fiddled with the radio. I felt confident I was heading in the right direction. Things were looking up.

Something thudded against the hood of my car. I jerked the steering wheel and the Impala fishtailed as I slammed on the brakes. We skidded sideways and the right rear tire hit a spruce tree, causing us to jerk to a stop.

"What." "The." "Shit?" I huffed. And then turned to face a wide-eyed Joseline. "You okay?"

When she nodded, I climbed out of the car. My knees wobbled and I had to lean on the vehicle to keep from crumpling to the ground. The dent in the car was massive.

Had it been a deer? I didn't see anything.

The woods around us were eerily still. No birdsong, I realized. That was odd. Like the forest was holding its breath.

I gestured for Joseline to get out of the vehicle. I'd

seen too many movies where a car exploded after being in an accident. Even though I doubted that my Impala was about to spontaneously combust, I wasn't about to risk her life. What I knew about cars could fit in a shot glass, with room enough for a slug of moonshine.

"Do you smell anything?" I asked the werewolf girl.

She lifted her nose and dragged in a breath. Frowned, and then wrinkled her nose.

"Something bad?"

She nodded and pointed off to the side of the road, where it ended.

Maybe the deer I'd hit had stumbled over the edge of the drop-off. That was an uneasy thought. I wondered if I ought to go over and see if it was still alive.

And then what? Use my newfound gift of comeuppance and throw myself in front of a car? I didn't carry a gun or a knife and wasn't the sort capable of putting the poor creature out of its misery.

The sound of gravel crunching under tires pulled me away from my dark thoughts. A black SUV appeared around the turn heading in the same direction I'd been traveling before the incident.

The vehicle slowed to a stop and the driver's window slid down. "Is everything all right?"

I swallowed. "No, actually. I think I hit a deer and I'm worried it's still alive and wounded."

"Where?" The man asked. He had dark hair and eyes and offered me a reassuring smile.

I pointed to the spot where the accident had occurred. The newcomer put on his hazard lights before climbing from the SUV. He strode to the side and looked down.

"Is it dead?" I asked anxiously, not wanting to see.

He nodded, not tearing his gaze away. "Oh yes. He's dead."

I made a face. "At least he's not suffering any longer."

The dark man straightened and slid his gaze to me. "My name is Declan. Where are you headed? Maybe I can give you a lift."

When I told him, he laughed. "What a coincidence. I own the hotel. This must be your lucky day."

CHAPTER 12
DONNA

"Is it just you?" The man, Declan he'd said his name was, asked.

"Just the two of us...." I trailed off when I realized that Joseline was gone. I turned in a circle like a dopey dog chasing her tail. "She was here a minute ago."

"I didn't see anyone." Declan offered me a soft smile.

"A little girl. She's thirteen." Why had Joseline run away? Had she needed to shift? Damn it, I should have been paying closer attention to her.

"She can't have gone far," Declan said in a soothing tone. "The hotel is right over the next rise. She probably went exploring. Let's get you all checked in and then I can help you look for her.

His words... I wanted to protest, to tell him that Joseline needed me and I had to find her now. But something about the cadence of his voice lulled and compelled me forward, into his SUV.

The vehicle smelled of new car. The leather was butter soft under my hands. As though in a daze I watched Declan unload my bags and place them in the back of his SUV. My head turned toward the trees and I thought I saw a wolf standing there, watching me. Wait was that....

Declan slid behind the wheel and turned to face me. His every molecule commanded my attention. "Buckle your seatbelt, Donna."

"Did I tell you my name?" I asked, even as my hands obeyed. I had to do what he said. It was important. I didn't know why only that it was necessary.

"No, but I know your sister," he said. "Process of elimination."

"Everyone knows my sister." I sighed. "Everyone but me."

Now, why had I said that? I wasn't the sort of person who opened up to random people she'd just met.

He shifted into drive and we drove away, leaving the wolf behind.

Declan had been right. His hotel sat atop the next rise. I felt a little loopy as he pulled up in front of the building and was grateful when he circled the car and led me into the hotel. It was beautiful. Limestone floors covered with oriental rugs. The check-in desk was stained mahogany. In the lobby, antique furnishings were artfully placed. Not so cluttered to make the space unusable. Oversized windows showed a view down over the lake. The overall vibe was warm and welcoming. I appreciated it after Storm Grove's coldness. Instead of heading for guest services, he strode to the antique elevator with an honest-to-goddess elevator operator standing sentinel before it.

"My suite," Declan said to the stranger in a brisk tone.

I wanted to correct him, to tell him that I wanted a cabin near the woods. But he turned to me, those dark eyes flickering with something that looked like flames, and said, "Hush."

My lips pressed together.

Wrong. Somewhere in the back of my mind, I was screaming that this wasn't right. I wasn't the sort of woman who blindly took orders. I tried to catch the elevator operator's attention, but the man kept his eyes on his work.

When the elevator doors dinged open, Declan propelled me forward by my arm into a carpeted hallway. "See to it we aren't disturbed," he said.

I wanted to argue but was still being compelled to hush. My pulse pounded in my ears and my mouth had gone dry. Too late, I recalled one of Grand's warnings.

"*Once you come into your powers, others can sense them in you. And many would steal what you possess, even though it means your life.*"

Declan said he knew Bella. Did that mean he was a member of a rival coven? No, because the hotel was located in Shadow Cove and that was Sanders's territory.

The hallway ended at a heavy mahogany door. There was a plate beside the door and Declan pressed his thumb against it. He smirked when he saw me watching him.

"Pretty high-tech for this old place. It is a bit of overkill but I just love the marriage of old and new." He opened the door and said, "Go in."

I went. And the scent hit me. It was embedded in the wood and plaster, and fabrics of the well-appointed suit.

Brimstone. *Oh shit.*

I took a deep breath and turned to face the demon my sister had summoned. "How do you hide your scent?"

Declan shrugged. "It fades the longer I remain on this plane. Only shifter noses are strong enough to detect it on me now. This was the first place I stayed when Bella released me from her circle. I'm afraid the scent embedded itself. You get used to it after a while."

This time I saw the flames as they blazed to life in his midnight eyes.

"Now, Donna Sanders Allen. You're going to tell me exactly what it is you are doing here."

Bella

KENDRA and I met at the bunkhouse.

"Anything?" I asked her. I'd checked the mirror a few hours earlier but there hadn't been any sign of a wraith. I was almost sorry.

"Not since yesterday." Kendra flipped the steak she'd been browning. "You hungry?"

I shook my head. My insides felt queasy, though I figured it was from stress more than the pregnancy.

"You need to take better care of yourself," Kendra said as she moved the steak to a platter. "You do good work, Bella. But those babies are going to demand a lot from you."

"Did you ever have any kids?"

"No." She shrugged and tucked into her breakfast. "But I taught preschool and Sunday school before I was turned, so I spent a lot of time with children. They're little energy vampires and will drain you dry."

The sound of snapping branches pulled our attention to the north woods. A moment later a small werewolf barreled out of the trees, heading straight for us.

"Joseline?" I asked as Kendra caught the girl up in her arms. "Why isn't she with Donna?"

It had been some measure of relief to know that my sister had a werewolf guarding her back. Even a young werewolf. But if Joseline was here…

Kendra frowned, her brows pulled together and I could tell she was struggling to make sense out of whatever images Joseline was sending her through the pack bonds. "There was a car accident."

My breath caught. "Is Donna hurt?"

"Not from what I can tell. I see Donna in an SUV with a man."

Joseline yipped.

"Didn't smell right?" Kendra cocked her head. "What did he smell like?"

Joseline whimpered and squirmed and Kendra set her down. "She doesn't know how to describe it. Just that he smelled rotten."

Cold curdled in my belly and I headed for the DeVille. "Keep an eye on her."

"Where are you going?" Kendra asked

I didn't answer, just maneuvered my bulk behind the steering wheel.

A werewolf who'd never encountered the scent of brimstone before might not know what that meant. But they had a natural aversion to the smell all demons carried.

"Damn it, Donna," I thought as I headed out onto the road that led to Declan's hotel. "Right from the frying pan and into the fire."

Declan couldn't hurt me. I was his summoner. But that protection wouldn't extend to my sister. At best, he now had leverage over me. He could force me into signing the blood contract, one that allowed him even more freedom.

At worst….

No, I wasn't going to think the worst. Donna would be all right. She had to be. I needed her.

Donna

"Can I get you a drink?" The demon asked me. He shucked his coat over the arm of a wingback chair and headed toward the kitchen.

"Huh?" Okay, not the most brilliant retort. Bella probably would have gone up one side of him and down the other. But the creature that called himself Declan had compelled me into this space. Hospitality was the absolute last thing I expected.

He returned carrying two crystal glasses full of a clear liquid that smelled of juniper berries.

I eyed mine dubiously.

"Oh come now," Declan said and swapped his glass with mine. "I can compel your feeble little mortal mind at will. Why would I bother drugging you?"

Point to the demon. Still, I set the glass on a bookshelf. "It's a little early in the day for me." Plus the reek of brimstone killed my desire to ingest anything.

"Suit yourself." The demon knocked back his drink and then picked up my abandoned one. "You'll have to forgive the compulsion spell, but I needed to get you behind my wards before another wraith attacked. I sensed you would put up a fuss about the wolf girl."

Joseline. With my wonky mind free once more, I headed for the door. "I need to find her—"

The demon moved with preternatural speed to block my path. I had to stop or slam into him. "She's safe. Headed right back to Storm Grove. It's only five miles as the crow flies to the west of this bluff. My guess is she's there by now, getting "help.""

Meaning Bella would be on her way. I swallowed and stared into those burning eyes and asked the question that I hadn't wanted to ask my sister. "Are you the father of her twins?"

Declan stepped away from the door. Probably sensing that I wasn't going to run. Instead, he knocked back the second drink. "How much do you know about my kind?"

"Demons?" I shook my head. "I know that supposedly you control the wraiths that enter sleeping souls and take over their mortal bodies." I didn't add that up until the incident at the portal I hadn't believed wraiths existed.

That man that Bella had burned. That we had burned...A shudder went through me and I wrapped my arms around myself as I remembered his blank gaze.

Declan snorted. "That's it? We control wraiths? That's the best the Sanders family of legacy witches can come up with? No wonder your sister summoned me. She didn't know any better."

"Hey," I snapped. "Up until yesterday, I thought I was a dud, okay? Demonology was lumped in with higher level magics, which I was never taught."

His brows drew together and he studied me closely. "Only a fool would mistake you for a dud, Donna Sanders-Allen. You're lucky I found you before that psychotic witch Vera Bradbury sniffed you out. She would have siphoned the powers right out of you."

"Siphoned?" I shook my head at the unfamiliar term. "What does that mean?"

Declan sighed. "If I'm going to be responsible for your entire higher education in the dark arts, we can at least be comfortable." He strode around the couch and plopped down, kicking his feet up on the coffee table and slinging one arm along the back cushion.

I hesitated. Was I supposed to trust the information given to me by the demon my sister summoned?

Then again, other than the compulsion, which he'd apologized for, he hadn't done anything heinous. I circled the couch as well, though I selected a low club chair so I sat at a diagonal from Declan.

"Demons, as we exist in the hell realm, are without gender or reproductive organs. It takes us several months in this realm to grow those organs. Most of us aren't here long enough for it to matter. But it would take years for one of us to be able to sexually procreate."

My mouth fell open even as my gaze went involuntarily to his lap. "So you don't have a—"

The demon reached forward and with two fingers, closed my mouth. "It's rude to ask about other beings' sexual organs. Didn't your mother teach you that?"

"My mother left when I was a teenager." I said.

His gaze was almost sympathetic. "Apologies."

I retrenched. "You were saying something about siphoners?"

"You know about dark fae and other magic hunters, yes?" At my nod, he continued. "Well, those groups were officially sanctioned by the magical council to take magic from unsanctioned practitioners by any means necessary. As a legacy, you and members of your family are sanctioned to practice from the moment of your birth until you draw your final breath. Officially."

I didn't like the blaze of flames in his eyes. "And unofficially?"

"Unofficially, your magic can be siphoned from you, even used against you by the ones who know how."

I jolted. "Witches actually, do that? Steal magic from each other?"

"For one of your advanced age you are woefully naive," Declan smirked when I glared at him. "You and Bella haven't had to deal with siphoners much. Your family's relative isolation and individual strength are enough to keep most of the bottom feeders from even trying. But your magic, Donna, is fresh. Unmarked by experience. Magic grows calloused after years of being bonded to the same soul. Tough to wrestle and harder to bend to a new practitioner's will. Others will make unholy alliances to steal your gifts. You might as well have hung out an open for business sign."

I swallowed as I recalled Annabeth's words from earlier. *"You've freed your magic but you've fastened a target on your back."* Was siphoning what she'd been talking about?

"We're getting off track," I said because I didn't want to think about hoards of unscrupulous magic users banding together to steal pieces of my soul. "Why did my sister summon you?" I began but was interrupted when the door burst inward.

Bella, hair flying, eyes like mirrors strode into the room. A blast of psychic power surged from her and hit Declan square in the chest.

The demon flew backward and crashed against the wall.

"Bella," I shouted but I could tell she couldn't hear me, all her focus was on the demon.

"You want my sister, you prick. You'll have to go through me first."

CHAPTER 13
BELLA

onna had run to my side, was pulling at my arm, and shrieked. "Stop! Stop it!" over and over again.

But I was in no mood to listen. I didn't have the kind of power required to stop a demon. While I could reflect a mortal or even a supernatural being and bend them to my will, demons were something different. I had to try, though. For Donna's sake.

With magic coursing through my bloodstream, she couldn't budge me, couldn't do anything while I focused on my target. And Declan....

The demon was laughing at me, even as his eyes blazed with the promise of hell. "Foreplay, witchling? In your condition?"

He threw up a shield, cutting my magic off mid-flow. I hissed as the intense pins and needles sensation of unspent magic rebounded onto me, through me. I was the conductor and on the demon's home turf. I wasn't grounded well enough to absorb the backlash. My belly tightened and I cried out more out of fear than pain.

As suddenly as the backlash had struck, it was cut off. I fell to my hands and knees, my entire body trembling, every cell lit up like I'd been struck by lightning.

"What did you do?" I heard Donna hiss and was gratified to hear the venom in her voice. She might not be able to stop Declan without me, but at least she wasn't under his spell.

Another jolt made my arms turn to jelly and I collapsed. My mind shrieked, *The girls! You have to protect the girls!* My body wasn't responding to the panicked signals. I would have landed on my rounded belly if strong hands hadn't caught me.

"There now, my fierce little summoner," the demon crooned as he turned me onto my side, so my head rested in his lap. His hand slid over my belly. "You are all right and so are our girls."

I wanted to shove him away. Not that his touch was revolting. The exact opposite. It felt too good to be held by him.

Evil was seductive. If it wasn't no one would succumb to temptation.

"Our girls?" Donna was the one to shove him back, to shift me from Declan's lap into her own. "You just said—"

"I said I didn't sire the babes," Declan snarled. "But possession is nine-tenths of the law. And one of those children belongs to me. Or it will after it breathes the air of this realm for the first time."

"Don't," I moaned. Even my words sounded garbled after the magical rebound.

"Don't what?" The demon crooned. "Tell her the truth? Tell your sister, your twin, that you were so desperate to enact revenge on your attacker that you promised me anything if I would do the deed?"

Dead silence.

Tears spilled down my face as I looked up at Donna. Shame burned hotter than the flames in the demon's eyes. I felt the need to apologize. To her, to my girls, hell, even to the demon. I'd made such a mess of everything.

Donna's green eyes were tear bright. "Is this true?"

What could I say? I could lie to the rest of the world. Maybe even to myself. But not my twin. "Yes," I croaked.

She let out a shuddering breath. "Oh, Bella. What happened?"

I jerked my head from side to side. I couldn't discuss it, not in front of Declan. He held enough of my secrets. I refused to show weakness in front of the enemy. Not if I wanted a fighting chance in hell of annulling our bargain.

"Get out," Donna snarled. For a moment I thought she might be talking to me before I realized she meant Declan.

To his credit, the demon rose to go. Why? Because he'd outed my shame? Hurting people was what demons did, why they were the bogymen, the supernatural assassins that our kind feared.

He swallowed and I saw the flames in his eyes die down as he looked at me. His expression was one of genuine remorse. He wasn't supposed to harm his summoner, not before the blood contract had been signed. But something made me think that maybe it was more than that.

Could demons feel regret?

"Out," Donna snapped.

The demon slunk off like a whipped dog. The door shut behind him with a small snick.

"Why don't you talk to Lewis like that?" I asked my sister. "He wouldn't know what hit him."

Donna ran a hand through her hair. "Honestly? I never wanted him to see this side of me."

"The bossy side?" My voice shook but bantering with her brought me down from the adrenaline spike. "How did you manage to hide it from him for all those years?"

Donna made a face as she helped me to my feet. "Not that. The intensity, the hyperfocus that comes with ADHD. I can be so goal driven that I don't pay attention to the collateral damage. Until it's too late."

I let out a breath when my legs held my weight. That was probably the closest I was ever going to get to an apology from my stubborn sister. "I need to sit down."

Ignoring the plaster dust that fell from my clothes, I sank onto the couch.

Donna poured a glass of water and brought it over to me. She spoke one word. "Who?"

The time for dodging questions was through. Donna's superpower, her hyperfocus, was fixed on me.

"Zeke Bradbury."

"Bradbury," She frowned and then blinked. "Of the Bradbury clan two towns over?"

I grimaced. The Bradburys had been rivals of the

Sanders family since our Grand had been young. We'd grown up hearing how backward and inbred the line was.

"It's not like you're thinking," I murmured.

"The demon said you were attacked. Did he mean rape?" Donna asked.

My throat closed. Talk about an ugly four-letter word. *Rape.* I'd never said it out loud. "It's complicated."

I'd expected her to snap and snarl and demand answers. Instead, she threaded her fingers through mine. "I have nowhere to be."

"That must be a first." I strove for a light tone but the way my twin looked at me made it clear it hadn't worked.

"After you...shut me out of your life last year, I met Zeke. He didn't tell me his last name. And I didn't ask."

Donna squeezed my hand but didn't speak. Good. It was difficult enough reliving my mistakes without constant questions.

"It was super casual. I didn't think he knew who I was and it was so freeing being something other than a legacy witch. We did normal stuff together. Went to movies or out to dinner. It was just the distraction I needed. Even when he fessed up that he was a warlock too, and that he was a Bradbury, I didn't think it was a big deal. Grand didn't know all the Bradburys, only Vera. Zeke seemed decent up to that point. I... trusted him."

The memory was so potent as it washed over me like a wave at the beach. I could still smell the stale beer, and feel the sticky floor beneath my shoes. We'd been out on a pub crawl. I'd had too much to drink and was leaning heavily on Zeke's arm.

"Take me back to your place," he'd murmured in my ear.

I'd jolted as I felt the thread of influence he'd wound around me. "It was nothing compared to a demon's compulsion spell and even tipsy, I'd been able to break free as easily as I could walk through a cobweb.

"He tried to laugh it off. Said he wanted me too badly to not tap into his magic. I was upset though and said I'd call an uber. He backed right off and I went outside to wait."

Donna was holding her breath as though she knew what was coming. Maybe she did. It was a twin thing.

"The uber showed up. I got in. But, I hadn't been paying attention to where I was. The driver was Zeke's cousin. And instead of bringing me home, he brought me to a cabin in the woods."

A tear rolled down my cheek. "Zeke was waiting for us. I tried to fight them off, Donna. I've thought about it over and over. I hadn't had that much to drink. Zeke must have slipped me something. And once I crossed into their territory, their wards kept my powers locked down. They took turns holding me down."

More images, the scent of male sweat. The tearing sound of my clothes being shredded. The tug of invisible hands pinning my arms, parting my thighs.

"They took turns...." My voice died just as Donna made a pained sound and wrapped her arms around me. I choked as I relived it in my mind. The pain, the rage, the fear. They planned it from the beginning. Targeted me."

"Not your fault," Donna was saying. "Bella, do you

hear me? This wasn't your fault."

Stars above, I wanted to believe her. Needed to, for the sake of my sanity.

She was rubbing my back. "How did you get away?"

I let out a shaky breath. "Once the drug wore off, I broke through their wards and reached for my magic. It wasn't as potent as usual, but I was able to call a sleeping spell long enough that I could get out of there." I'd had to walk back to the bar.

"That was the night I'd met Axel. He was closing up right as I arrived. He took one look at me and I knew he could tell what had happened. But he was Axel, so he just asked if he could help. He called Kendra and she came and picked me up. A few weeks later, I went back and offered him a job as my personal assistant."

"And you never went to the police? Or the hospital?" Donna asked.

I shook my head. "I can't send mortals up against warlocks. And there are too many Bradburys and only one of me."

Donna squeezed my hand again. "Is that why you summoned the demon? For revenge?"

My teeth sank into my lower lip and I gave a slow nod. "That was before I knew I was pregnant. I had no idea what he would ask for. I thought maybe a family heirloom or an expensive amulet. A healing spell. I summoned him in a fit of drunken rage. But we hadn't agreed on terms. I didn't sign the blood contract."

"And he wants a baby." Donna laid her head back against the couch and then rolled her head to face me. "How do you plan to get rid of him?"

"I'm still working on it," I said. "For a while I was wondering if he wasn't the one sending the wraiths to the portal, to keep me distracted. But he says no."

"And you believe him?"

Wordlessly, I nodded.

Her throat bobbed and I saw her swallow. "Can I ask you a question?"

"Why am I keeping them?" I asked and caressed my stomach.

Her gaze searched my features. "You don't have to—"

"This could be my only chance to be a mother." I shut my eyes. "That's what I realized when Grand died. That I'm in my forties and have never bothered living. You were right about that. Meeting someone, falling in love, having kids. I wanted all those things but I never pursued them. I've just been guarding the portal for my whole life. I'm forty-five, Donna. Who knows how much longer I have before the clock runs out? And these babies, no matter how they got here, are mine." Conviction rang in my words and I opened my eyes so I could read her expression.

She looked.... sad.

"The ultimate career woman." Donna smiled but it died a quick death. "How did you know I was here, Bells?"

I let her change the subject. "Joseline showed up at the bunkhouse. Told us where you were."

Donna stiffened. "Is she all right?"

"Physically, yeah. She didn't like seeing a demon compel you into his car right after you killed a man."

My sister froze. "What?"

"You hit someone. Probably a wraith-ridden someone. I spotted the body on my way here when I saw your car. Don't worry, Declan will take care of it."

"He won't like...eat it, will he?" she shuddered.

"Those were just stories Grand made up to scare us so we didn't muck about with the portal." At least I hoped they were. According to Annabeth, no one had disappeared under mysterious circumstances since I'd summoned the demon. I had to conclude that he wasn't keeping up a steady diet of human flesh.

"Another dead man." She leaned her head back on the couch. "What the fuck is happening, Bella?"

"I wish I knew."

She rolled her head along the cushion until she could look at me. Her gaze dropped to my belly. "Are you sure you're okay? Should I take you to the hospital? Or summon the healer?"

"They won't come here. Declan has the place warded against witches."

"Then what are we doing here?"

I shook my head. "Maybe because I'm his summoner?"

"That didn't keep him from tossing you around like a rag doll." My sister's eyes took on that hint of emerald fire I'd seen the night before when she'd faced her scumbag husband. "He'll pay for it, too."

"No," I gripped her arm. "Donna, listen to me. You can not use comeuppance against the demon."

"Why not?" Her chin tilted to a stubborn angle.

"Because it won't work the way it's meant to. Demons have protection against all witch gifts. A natural

155

immunity. It'll only piss him off more. And you don't have the protection of being his summoner." I finished the water and set the glass aside. "I'm exhausted."

"Then let's get you home." She helped me to my feet.

"Are you coming with me?"

Donna nodded. "I guess I don't have much of a choice. Not if wraith-ridden mortals or siphoners are going to fling themselves in front of my damn car every time I leave the property."

"Siphoners?" I asked.

She tugged me to the door. "I'll explain on the way."

The demon was lurking in the corridor and his burning gaze went to me as we approached.

"Bella," he began.

"Don't," I barked with the ring of command in my voice. He froze, every muscle in his glamoured body locking. "We're leaving. Don't follow us."

"I didn't mean to—"

I rounded on him. "You're supposed to protect me from my attackers, not attack me yourself!"

He recoiled and I turned back to where Donna stood, those green eyes taking us all in.

I didn't let out the breath I was holding until the elevator doors closed behind us.

Donna

THIS ONE *I can't blame on Bella,* I thought as I stared down at the dead man that had crossed in front of my car. Wraith-ridden or not, demon food or not, his blood was on my hands. As well as my fender.

"Think of it this way," Bella said from her position behind the wheel of her DeVille. She was wearing over-sized sunglasses so I couldn't see her eyes. "The more of them we take out, the better the parking around town will be."

"You're sick," I told her.

"I'm practical," she returned like we were the Williams sisters at Wimbledon. "He was trying to attack you, Donna. Whether he was one of these siphons or wraith-ridden, he came for you. And you defended your-self. It's that simple."

How could she say that? "This was someone's life," I protested.

"What did Grand always say? Survival of the fittest goes double for legacies. We don't become legacies by letting the chaff take us out."

"I hit him with my car," I snapped. "I thought he was a deer for fuck's sake."

"And you don't think that's comeuppance at work?" She pointed to the gorge. "He acted like an animal so he died like one."

I shook my head. "But I didn't do anything. I didn't even know he was attacking me until after it was over."

My sister removed her glasses and just stared at me. "Don't you remember any of the lessons on legacy magic? We're different because our magic will seek out harm before it lands on our doorstep. It is cultivated over generations to take care of the problem before we even know we have it. That's why we have to trust in it completely. Trust in who and what we are. Believe that there is a reason for everything that happens, no matter what."

Her hand flitted over her stomach as she said the last three words. I was still trying to process it all. My sister had summoned a demon to …protect her. From the Bradbury clan, two of whom had raped her.

There was more to the story, but this wasn't the time or the place to wheedle it out of her. Even if Bella was in the mood to talk, which judging by the look on her face, she wasn't.

I studied my Impala. Other than the bloody dent— shudder—it was probably drivable. Still, I didn't want to leave hard evidence for the police to find in case someone was looking for the man. "Can you magic this back to the way it was before the accident?"

"I can." She was staring blankly out her windshield. "But it would be better practice for you."

I blew out a sigh. "Bella, I don't have time—"

"For what? For me? For magic? Make the fucking time, Donna. This is more important than your divorce or your clients or anything else. You working with your magic might mean the difference between us living or dying. And that includes my girls."

I wanted to bark at her, to insist that my life wasn't frivolous and that what I did was important. It was, I believed that down to my marrow. My gaze slid to the blood-encrusted metal. Just not as important as our survival.

"You're right," I said with a sigh. "What do I do?"

"Do you remember the spell for returning objects to their original state?"

"Vaguely." I'd studied all the basic spells alongside my sister. Preparing for the day when my power would emerge and I would be able to wield all the energies of the universe. Grand had insisted. Dud or not, I had been schooled in legacy witchcraft including elemental magic and cover-up spells.

At Bella's level, the words to the spell were no longer necessary. She could call fire, water, minerals, and air to do her bidding. But she'd learned to do that by chanting the words, learning to draw energy through herself. The chants helped us focus our minds where they needed to be.

"Good, now think the words. Say them out loud if you need to and imagine the outcome. And close your eyes. Picture what you want to happen if you can."

"And if I can't?" I didn't always see things in words or images but in colors, and feelings.

"Don't worry about what you can't do," Bella advised. "Focus on what you can do and the need you have to do it."

Taking a deep breath, I shut my eyes and began the chant. This at least felt familiar. I'd spent half of my waking hours from ages six to nine with my eyes closed, learning the spells that were the foundations for our craft. Bella was right alongside me. And even after her reflection gift emerged, we still took lessons together. I heard her voice, not in my ears but in my memory.

Sun, wind, rain, and fire
Feel the need that is most dire
Return this object to its previous state
Allow this witch a clean slate.

I said it three times. Three and seven were numbers steeped in magic. Three was the primary number for establishing balance, like the legs on a stool. Seven was the number of those who took a spiritual path, overcame obstacles, and persevered through life's mysteries to reach the ultimate state of ecstasy. Like the term seventh heaven. I didn't need the big guns for this spell, so I figured a three-chant would be best.

Just as when I'd been a kid, I felt nothing. No heat or flare of energy, nothing like Bella's outward displays of power. My wonky brain started to worry that I was doing something wrong but I hushed it. Bella would correct me if the need arose. When I opened my eyes, the silver quarter panel gleamed in the late afternoon sun, and not even a scuff was visible.

"It worked!" A huge grin felt as though it would split my face. I had never intentionally worked magic before. Elation coursed through me.

"It's about time," My sister murmured. "Now, let's go home."

My lips parted and I wanted to tell her it wasn't my home, not anymore, but then stopped when I saw the look on her face.

"Okay, Bella. Let's get you home."

CHAPTER 14
DONNA

T'd been all set to have a chat with Bella but she'd pulled over along the side of the road before we headed up to the house.

"I need to go back to the portal," she said. "I want to check something."

"I'll come with you," I offered but she'd shaken her head.

"No, go up to the house. I'll be there in ten minutes or so."

An hour later she still hadn't returned.

I paced the length of the kitchen as Axel sliced into a London broil. "Where the hell is she? And why isn't she answering her phone?"

"She might have lost it again," Axel said.

I blinked up at him. "Again? She's lost her phone before?"

"At least twice since I've been here."

"Son of a bitch," I cussed and then whirled on my heel, almost tripping over the werewolf who was lying in the doorway. "Sorry, sweets. I need to go into Bella's room for a bit. Wait for me here, okay?"

In answer, she sprawled on her side on the floor.

I headed into the ground floor suite and took it in with new eyes. The clothes were strewn every which way. The unmade bed. The hodgepodge of witchy items on the vanity and windowsills. Charms and amulets hanging off of lampshades and out of dresser drawers. Her confession about buying me clothes.

My throat clogged as I approached the desk. Stared at the pile of unopened mail.

Axel took care of the rest of the house. But Bella's room, the room she'd taken over when Grand had died, was her sanctuary.

And in a way, her prison.

I closed my eyes and sank heavily into a chair. Of course. Of frigging course. Why hadn't I seen it before?

We were twins. Genetic matches. Like Lewis had said, two peas in a pod. I had magic and Bella...

I heard the door open and felt her presence. Turned to look at her.

"Lost track of time?" I asked mildly.

She stared at me for a long moment.

"Yeah, I do that one too. I keep thinking I can fix it if I will it hard enough. I mean shit, I have magic now and everything. Yet still not a fucking timelord. The universe's cruel joke. I've learned the hard way not to book a place that charges you if you're more than fifteen minutes late. They call it the ADHD tax."

Bella swallowed visibly.

"Why didn't you tell me?" I whispered.

"I haven't been officially diagnosed."

I wanted to stare at her open-mouthed or shake my head. But that was the absolute worst thing I could have done. Bella didn't need my judgment or my shame. She had more than enough of her own.

Slowly, I got to my feet and headed to her. Taking a page out of Axel's book I wrapped my arms around her and held her close.

"It'll be all right," I told my sister. "You aren't alone anymore."

She broke. Her arms went tight about me and she held on for dear life. Her body trembled as she sobbed, letting all the fear and frustration, and shame out of her head and her heart.

And I took it all. Because I knew what it was like to be alone and dealing with this. Of hearing people ask what was wrong with you and knowing deep down that something really was different. Something set you apart from the rest. In a bad way. A way that left you feeling lost, helpless, and hopeless. It wasn't just the burden of being a legacy witch. It was the struggle of adulting without the damn user's manual.

"It's okay," I told my sister. "I'm here now. And we will sort your shit out. I promise."

She took a shuddering sigh and then pulled back. "You mean it?"

At my nod, she seemed to deflate.

"I love you, Bells." It had been too long since I'd said that to her.

"I love you too." She sagged onto the chair.

"Is that why you hired Axel?" I asked. "To help control the chaos?"

She nodded and wiped her wet green eyes with her sleeve. "Yeah, he's great."

I waved to the mail. "And is he getting paid?"

Her teeth sank into her lower lip. "I'm not sure when the last time was."

I let out a sigh. "Okay. The first thing you're going to do is go take a shower. Because between you, me, and the wall, you are ripe."

Her mouth kicked up. "Those who live in glass houses?"

I sniffed and then wrinkled my nose. "It's the demon funk more than me. So yeah, if the old ass water heater can take it, I'll wash too. And then we'll eat."

"And then?" she whispered.

"Then we'll talk." I let out a long breath. "It's long overdue."

Bella smiled and rose. She didn't waddle the way I had done when I was pregnant but glided. She touched me on the shoulder. "Out of curiosity, before today who did you think fathered my babes?"

Heat suffused my cheeks. "Um... well, you moved Axel in here very quickly and he is really cute,"

She cast me a withering glance. "Donna, puppies are cute. Axel is five alarm hotness.'"

I shifted from foot to foot. "Does that mean you've slept with him?"

Bella answered my question with one of her own. "Would it matter if I had?"

"Yes!" I said.

"I guess you'll never know then." She smirked at me and sauntered off to the bathroom.

"Witch!" I called after her and then put my face in my hands. "What the hell are you thinking, Donna? He's too young. You're still married. It shouldn't matter."

But it did, damn it. She was my sister and we lived by one hard and fast rule, no poaching. Not even exes. And though I was trying I couldn't get those blazing hot kisses out of my head.

⚔

Bella

WHEN DONNA HAD SAID we I thought she meant the two of us. But after she helped Axel clear the table, something I wouldn't have ever thought to do, she gestured for him to join us. Joseline, still in wolf form, slept on a rug by the stove, obviously unwilling to let my sister out of her sight.

"When was the last time you got paid," my sister asked my PA bluntly.

He frowned. "I'm not here for the money."

Donna made a sweeping gesture with her hand. "That's not what I asked. We're trying to sort some things out and we'll be leaning heavily on you to do it. I want you to know you can trust us."

He swallowed and then gave me a tight smile. "About three months ago."

My jaw dropped. That meant half the time he'd been here he hadn't been paid. "And you didn't say anything?"

JENNIFER L. HART

He shrugged. "You have bigger things to worry about."

I just shook my head. How had it gone so wrong?

"That'll be the first task we're going to ask of you, Axel," Donna murmured. "Keep track of things like that. I'm amazed the electricity hasn't been shut off."

"Mom bought into the solar grid," I said. "We usually get a check this time of year, not a bill."

"Did you cash those checks?"

I shook my head, heat scalding my cheeks.

Donna nodded slowly. "Okay. What about property taxes? Credit card bills? You said you were buying me things and Storm Grove is a high-maintenance dame."

Axel cleared his throat. "I uh, had to pay in cash the other day at the farmer's market. The card you gave me for expenses was declined."

I moaned but Donna nodded as though she had expected it.

"We're gonna go cash only from here on out. I can't be trusted with a credit card either." She squeezed my hand.

We went over it all, item by item. Donna fetched the bag of mail from my room and made me open every last envelope. Axel sorted the checks from the bills from the statements and kept the tallies for each in a little notebook.

"This is humiliating," I said as I opened yet another envelope.

"Not as humiliating as having the power shut off to your house," my sister said grimly. "Lewis was so pissed every time he had to go down to the city office and pay the bill to get it turned back on. It's no wonder he started shopping out my replacement right when Devon left."

"Stop that," I snapped at the same time Axel growled, "He's an ass."

She blinked at both of us.

"You didn't do anything wrong, Donna," I told her with absolute conviction. "It isn't your fault."

She nodded, but her eyes were red-rimmed as she waved at the piles of papers. "I know. But who would want to sign on for living like this if they don't have to?"

She closed her eyes so she didn't see the look Axel was giving her. But I did. *That answers that question.*

"I think that's enough misery for one night," I said and pushed my chair away from the table.

Donna nodded and then forced a smile. "Okay. You're right. We'll do more tomorrow."

"What about your business proposal?" Axel asked her.

She slapped her palm to her forehead. "Yeah, that too. I forgot how easy it is to get sidelined in this house."

"Witches and demons and werewolves, oh my," I quipped and she laughed.

I got to my feet and had Donna and Axel on either side of me, lending a hand. "I got it," I told them both. "If I need help, I'll ask for it."

"Will you?" Donna whispered.

"Yeah," I said and hugged her. "Now, I will ask you if I need help, whether it's magic or mundane shit."

"I think I would prefer the magic," she said. "Night Bells."

I headed to my room, past the piles of items that still

needed to be dealt with, and crawled into bed. I'd just shut my eyes when I felt a slight tapping against one of my wards.

Declan.

The demon could bust through like the Kool-Aid man through a brick wall if he chose. The fact that he was asking permission rather than bludgeoning his way through was a nice change.

I dropped the ward. A moment later, smoke slithered through my open bedroom window. He materialized lying on his side facing me. He wore a black button-down shirt that was open three buttons and tailored slacks that fit his lean frame with ease.

"What are you doing here?" I asked.

"I wanted to make sure you're all right." Those midnight eyes searched my face.

"It was just a rebound spell," I shrugged. "No harm done."

"I wasn't talking about the spell."

I licked suddenly dry lips. "You mean am I going to send you back to your hell plane because you let the cat out of the bag to my sister that I was raped?"

He didn't flinch. I don't know why I'd expected him to. He was a demon. He'd seen the very worst the world had to offer.

"She needed to know," he said. "Keeping it a secret was only hurting you."

"Why do you even care?" I whispered.

His hand drifted to my stomach. It wasn't the posses-sive touch that he usually gave me, the one that made all the fine hairs on my neck stand on end. No, instead it was gentle, almost exploratory.

"It's not good for them," he said at length. Though I thought there might be more that he wasn't saying. I was too tired to puzzle it out though.

I yawned and then cleared my throat. "Well, you've seen for yourself that I'm all right. Feel free to let yourself out."

"I think I should stay," he murmured and flames flared in his dark eyes as he focused on my lips.

"Do you want the kiss I promised you?" I asked.

He shook his head. "Not yet."

What was he waiting for?

I drifted off before I could ask.

<hr/>

Donna

I STARED AT THE ROOM, utterly dumbfounded. It was empty.

Well, not entirely. The bed was still in the same place, though it had a puffy white comforter and new white pillows adorning it. There was an old rolltop desk painted an antique white and a matching ladder-back chair with a plush red cushion tied to it. An overstuffed armchair with a red throw draped over one arm sat by the window. Beside it, I spotted a basket full of paperbacks. A standing lamp with a shade decorated with cherries sat beside it.

But the best part was the French doors. I squealed with delight. It had been so long since I'd seen them, I'd forgotten they were even there. My footsteps were quick and light as I went for them and flung them wide, allowing the night air to spill into the small space.

"I'm guessing by that sound that you like it," Axel said from behind me.

I whirled to face him. "When did you do all this?"

"Earlier today."

"Even after I left?" I blinked.

He made a motion as though his shirt was too tight, an uncomfortable sort of shrug. "I told you I would do it. And I hoped...."

"What did you hope?" I shouldn't ask the question. We were intruding on dangerous ground.

But I really wanted to hear the answer.

His gray eyes were so soft in the moonlight as he looked at me. "I hoped that if I made a space for you, you would know you were wanted."

"Oh, Axel." A breathy sigh escaped. "What am I going to do with you?"

One eyebrow lifted. "Are you hunting for suggestions? Because I have a few. And they are all verbs."

A laugh bubbled out of me. True joy, the likes of which I hadn't felt since my son was small. Thinking of Devon sobered me right up.

"Axel," I began.

"Don't, Don."

"Don't what?"

"Say whatever it is you were about to say." He shook his head. "I know it's a long shot but I just want…I just want you to know that you're appreciated. I get the feeling that you haven't been for a very long time."

He wasn't wrong.

He held out a hand. "Dance with me?"

"Here?" I looked around automatically, but if anyone was watching, they were doing so through wolf eyes. "There's no music."

"And?"

Slowly I reached out and took his hand.

He took it and spun me in a circle. The move was so unexpected that I laughed out loud. He was grinning by the time he spun me back and dragged my body up next to his. The scent of nigh blooming jasmine washed over the two of us as we swayed together in the moonlight.

"I like seeing you this way," he murmured as we circled the terrace.

"What way is that?"

"Confident. Joyful." With that, he leaned forward. I held my breath, knowing he was going to kiss me again. And I was sure that I didn't have the strength to resist him.

He did kiss me. On the forehead. I watched as he strode from the room, shutting the door just as Joseline walked past him.

"Hey you," I said, glad to see she had once again decided to retake her human form.

She held out the bottle of avocado oil and the scarf

I'd used to wrap her hair the night before in silent request.

"You got it." I moved into the space and made to shut the doors when a small voice said,

"Could you leave them open?"

I froze. Not wanting to make a big deal out of it, I turned away from the door and pulled out the chair for her. "Sure thing. Same as last night?"

At her nod, I set to the task. I wanted to apologize for what happened. In retrospect, it was my impulsiveness more than anything else that had driven me away that morning. And I'd drug this traumatized girl along in my wake, telling myself and everyone around us that she would be better anywhere but here. That was my damage though, Storm Grove was my bane.

Or it had been. Before Axel.

The truth was though that Joseline was a werewolf. And she needed to be around people who understood her. The same way Bella needed me.

"He likes you," she whispered when I was about halfway through her hair.

"Who?" I knew very well who, I just wanted to keep her talking.

"Axel." She smiled up at me. "He's very handsome."

"That he is."

"And he saved me."

I paused. "Sounds like maybe you like him."

"I do, but not the way he likes you. He's...nice. Talks to me the same way whether I'm like this or...the other way. And he makes very good food."

I finished with her hair and wiped my hands on a

towel. "That, darling girl, is the finest quality a man can possess."

"So do you like him?" She turned to look up at me with those curious dark eyes.

"It's complicated." Although what the fuck wasn't anymore?

She nodded, accepting my explanation, and yawned.

"Time for bed," I said and held the sheets up so she could slide underneath. "Want me to sleep on the floor?" I had the night before when I'd found her fast asleep.

She shook her head so I got into bed beside her and switched off the lamp.

"It's complicated," I whispered to the darkness before giving in to it.

CHAPTER 15

DONNA

If the dream came during the night, I didn't recall it. I awoke feeling refreshed and ready to start the day. Joseline was still asleep so I carried my laptop downstairs, intending to work out on the patio the way I'd seen Bella doing the day before. A little fresh air and sunlight would help clear out the cobwebs. And coffee. Gallons of it.

Axel stood at the counter wearing nothing but a pair of pajama bottoms. I froze at the sight. Not just because of his broad shoulders or taut muscles, but the scars. Long and curved along each shoulder blade.

Without thinking it through I moved up behind him and touched the puckered skin. "What happened here?"

He'd stiffened on contact but then relaxed when he saw it was me. "I don't know. They've been there all my life."

His skin was warm, almost hot to the touch. So many unanswered questions. His strength, the preternatural way he could move, the mystery of his past.

"Annabeth offered to find out about your past if I gave her some blood," I whispered.

He rounded, catching my wrist. "I hope you didn't take her up on it."

I shook my head. "I know better than to make bargains with her."

He nodded and then turned away. I saw him reach for a shirt. "You don't have to cover up on my account. I mean, it's going to be hot today."

My face felt flushed and I was sure my cheeks were scarlet. It sounded like I was propositioning him.

He flashed me a quicksilver smile. "Yeah, but I hear footsteps overhead. Don't want to ruin her for all other men."

I grinned and then headed to the fridge. The cool air blew on my overheated skin. Was this what a hot flash felt like?

"Let me get the kettle on for Bella's tea and I'll cook you something," Axel offered.

"You don't have to—" I turned away and was promptly backed into the stainless steel door.

"I want to take care of you." The words echoed through me with sensual promise. I'd hidden my heart away in the deepest darkest part of a hidden cavern and yet Axel had unearthed it and held it in his hand.

My mouth had gone dry. "You mean like the way you take care of Bella."

He frowned. "What are you talking about?"

Shit, was I really going to ask him this? I needed to know and Bella wouldn't divvy.

Looking up into his eyes I asked, "Have you slept with my sister?"

For a minute I didn't think he would answer. Then he doubled over, big body shaking as he laughed like a lunatic on nitrous oxide.

"It's not freaking funny!" I bristled like a scalded cat.

He couldn't speak, only waved a hand at me. "Can't breathe."

I huffed out a breath embarrassment making me pissy. "That's not a no. And it's a fucking deal breaker for me if you have!"

He sobered. Rose to his full height until he loomed over me and locked his gaze with mine. "You need to hear the words, Donna? Fine. No, I have never slept with your sister. We're friends. I look out for her. But it's you I want. Is that clear enough?"

"Your eyes," I whispered in awe.

Intensity radiated out of his every pore. "What about them?"

His gray irises flickered with what looked like forks of purple lightning. What sort of creature had eyes that changed that way? My hand hovered in midair. I wanted to touch him, to feel that intensity for myself.

His hands rested lightly on my shoulders and he lowered his lids. "Something is happening to me, Don. When I look at you or catch a whiff of your scent, I feel it... surfacing."

It. He talked about himself like it was part of another being that he struggled to contain. The impulse rose that I should glue myself to his side to see what would happen. But I couldn't. Bella needed my help and I wanted to get some answers out of her.

I put my hand over his chest, over where his heart was thumping wildly under his t-shirt. "It'll be okay. Whatever it is. How about I bring Bella her fungus tea? Give you a little space?"

His jaw clenched and I could see the effort it took for him to release me. But he did and then stepped away.

Rattled and more than a little hot and bothered, I scooped up Bella's cup, then breathing through my nose let myself into her bedroom.

"Oh, you've got to be shitting me," I snapped.

"What?" Bella sat up, hair a tangled mess.

"Impulse control, Bells. We have got to work on that one."

She stared at me blankly.

I pointed. "You're snuggled up with your demon."

Declan yawned and stretched. "What time is it? I have a Zoom meeting at nine."

At least the bastard was fully dressed. Curiosity aside, I really didn't want to see whatever he had going on downstairs. "It's a little after seven."

"Time enough for breakfast then? Have your domestic make some bacon. I find I am exceedingly fond of the stuff." Declan got out of bed and shuffled toward the bathroom.

"What are you thinking?" I hissed at my twin. "He attacked you yesterday and now I find you *spooning* with him?"

Bella

I GRIMACED. "In his defense, I went after him first."

"He's a *demon*." Donna put extra emphasis on the last word.

"I know."

Her brows drew together. "Wait, are you still worried about the Bradburys coming after you? Is that why the demon is here?"

"I came to apologize." The demon lurked in the doorway. "Isn't that the proper thing civilized beings do?"

Donna whirled around and I saw her hands come up. Here at the house, her magic was strong and highly focused. A rebound spell might kill her.

I threw myself out of bed and lurched in between them. My center of gravity was off and I would have fallen if Donna hadn't caught my left arm, just as Declan snagged my right.

"Bella," Donna bitched. "You need to be more careful!"

I tugged my arm free from hers so I could push my hair out of my face. "So do you. Donna, please give us a minute."

"But—"

I rounded on her. "I've got this."

She looked at me for a long minute, before glaring at Declan and stalking out of the room.

I'd let her take charge last night because my reserves had been depleted. Between reliving my attack and then the reveal of my probable ADHD, my system had been overloaded. But while Donna had devoted her life to simplifying and organizing and trying to function like a dud, I'd embraced the craft. Demons and magic were my realms of expertise. She would have to yield to me on occasion. Even if it chapped her ass.

"I'm growing on her," Declan murmured.

"Maybe like a rash." I shook my head. "I had to explain to her yesterday that you don't eat people."

Flames flared in his eyes. "Oh, I wouldn't go making promises on that front, witchling. I'm sure if the situation called for it, I could find certain people downright... tasty." His gaze caressed my body.

My lips parted and a puff of air escaped. "You're getting bolder."

"It's part of the territory. Less mindless killing machine that revels in blood and death. More like an animal with primitive urges. I find some things are beginning to appeal to me more than others. Watching over you while you slept, for instance." He tilted his head in that way that I'd come to think of as his considering look. "It...affected me strangely. It filled me with a new emotion. I believe mortals call it...satisfaction."

My toes curled. What was he saying?"

"I find myself reluctant to leave you now that I know you can be so vulnerable." He took a step closer to me and ran a finger over my collarbone. "Let me kill them for you."

"No." Terror flooded my system.

"Why? That's the reason you summoned me. Let me fulfill my purpose."

I just shook my head. "No, Azmodeous. I forbid you from killing those men."

JENNIFER L. HART

Those flames flared even brighter until his eyes were pits of fire. The hand moved up until his long digits were wrapped around my neck. "You think using my summoning name would stop me, witchling? You think I couldn't find a way around your demand if I put half a moment's thought into it?"

The heat radiating from him was just shy of blistering. I'd been so cold for so long that I reveled in the touch and swayed into him.

Shock replaced the threat that had twisted his features. "You're even more reckless than I believed. You play with fire, witchling."

I swallowed against his hold. "You won't hurt me. And not just because I'm your summoner."

His nostrils flared. I laughed.

"Look at you, demon. Nothing but a ridiculous tease. It's a good thing I have things to do today, otherwise, I'd compel you to put up or shut up."

"You don't mean it." He shook his head.

I lifted my chin at a challenging angle. "Want to bet?"

He stepped back. "No. I don't believe you. This is just another of your attempts to bend me to your will. It won't work. Do you hear me? I *will not* be manipulated."

Before I could respond, he faded to smoke. Those twin flames in his irises were the last to vanish.

I sagged back onto the mattress and tipped my head back. The demon was right. I was reckless. The impulse to call him out on all his teasing and sexual intimidation had washed over me. I'd been pretty sure Declan was all talk. Hell, he hadn't even been fully developed for most of

180

his time on this plane. The flirting was his way to communicate and make me uncomfortable. Throw me off my stride. And it had, just not in the way he had intended.

"Bella?" Axel called from the other side of the door. "Is your...um...guest staying for breakfast?"

"No," I raised my voice so he could hear me through the door. "No, he's gone."

My hand curved over my stomach. I had no doubt that he'd be back.

Donna

HYPERFOCUS ACTIVATED.

Sitting in the shade on the patio I buzzed through my research for Ali Smith's playroom conversion to a bedroom. I needed to get a GC out there to give me an estimate on bringing the space up to code, but the sex implements would find better homes. Cash in hand for Ms. Smith.

Thank the Goddess the internet and social media had connected all the perverts in striking distance. We'd clear the clutter in no time.

"Why are you looking up sex swings, Don?"

I snapped the laptop shut. Axel had chilled out from his earlier outburst and looked the same way he had the first time I saw him.

"I don't want to tell you," I murmured as he poured me more coffee without my having to ask. The man must be heaven-sent. "I'd get in trouble for corrupting a minor."

The skin around his eyes crinkled. "I'm not *that* young."

"Please. I have underwear older than you."

He just raised an eyebrow. "I'm twenty-five."

"And modern science tells us that the brain doesn't finish maturing until mid to late twenties." I sat back, confident I'd made my point.

"Why are you making such a big deal about my age?" His eyes narrowed. "Because you're insecure about yours?"

"I am not—" I spluttered and then retrenched. "I'll have you know that I am a well-preserved forty-five." Even though I never remembered to put on sunscreen. Sanders' genes were good for more than just magic.

"Who cares?"

I blinked at him.

Axel shrugged. "Age is just a number."

I made a disgusted sound. "You get to say that. You're a guy. Biology doesn't work the same way for us."

I thought about the sadness on Bella's face when she'd admitted that this pregnancy was probably her last chance. Men could spawn until their dying breath. And there was always another Mindy around to replace a woman who'd aged out of her baby-making years.

Even now I was struggling with perimenopausal hormone fluctuations and how they exacerbated my ADHD. What would that look like when full-blown menopause hit? And Goddess, poor Bella was dealing with pregnancy hormones.

"See, it sounds good to say that age is just a number," I told Axel. "Very modern and politically correct. But the reality is my body is going through changes similar to puberty in reverse. I wake up each day and wonder what fresh hell I'm going to be dealing with today. Hot flashes? Night sweats? Or maybe my favorite jeans will stop fitting because of all the carbs you're tempting me with. Maybe it'll be my wonky brain being even wonkier, like getting me lost in my hometown. Then there's my asshole husband throwing me over for a freaking zygote and locking me out of my house and having me arrested or—"

The words broke off on a sob and I covered my face with both hands. Or maybe I would have a massive mood swing in front of the very cute, very sweet guy whom I was developing a major crush on. Even though I knew better.

"Hey," Axel pried my hands away from my face, exposing my shame. "Don, it's okay. I know. It's been a lot. No wonder you're overwhelmed."

I'd unloaded on him with both barrels. That still didn't stop him from tugging me close or holding me while the storm of feelings raged. Wave after wave of emotion tossed me around as I finally took time to process everything that had happened. My life had changed drastically since I dropped Devon off at college. The betrayal was bad enough, but the way Lewis had handled everything made it so much worse. I felt like a horse that had been shipped off to the glue factory because I'd outlived my usefulness.

I sat back abruptly, wiping my eyes as realization dawned. "He always had such...contempt for me."

"Who?" Axel asked as he handed me the cloth napkin from the breakfast tray to wipe my eyes. "Your ex?"

Right, Axel wasn't inside my head, couldn't follow my thoughts. "Lewis, yes. Because of my ADHD. And because Bella is who she is and this is where I came from I was always...less than him. He would tell people that. 'Donna couldn't keep the house clean if her life depended on it.' He'd play it off like a big joke when we were out at parties or over to someone else's place for dinner. And I put up with it. For years."

My gaze drifted toward the pine forest. "I let him get away with it. The blatant disrespect. With not listening to me. With everything."

The wind picked up and blew my hair into my eyes. Axel reached out and tucked a strand behind one ear.

"I shouldn't have married him. But I was so tired of being the dud. Bella's less interesting, less beautiful twin."

"Who said something so ridiculous?" he asked.

I opened my mouth to tell him, but then shut it. I didn't have a name. Who had said it? Me. To myself. Every time Bella got a spell to work and mine flopped. Every time I caught some guy at school eyeballing my ethereal sister. Coveting her uniqueness and wishing I had a smidge of her charm.

"It's a story you've been telling yourself, isn't it?" Axel asked.

At my nod, he sat back. "That's the worst kind. Because with other people? We can shut them down, or tune them out. But when we tell ourselves this sort of shit, what choice do we have but to believe it?"

"That's... incredibly insightful, Axel."

He shrugged. "Told you. Age is just a number. It's the mileage that counts."

I laughed and it came out as a snort.

"Did you just snort laugh?"

"Shut up." I flushed, embarrassed.

"That's so cute."

What was it about this guy? He had me running the gauntlet of emotions in a matter of minutes. And he always saw me through and left me feeling better off on the other side.

"It's okay, Don." Axel touched my cheek. "You're out now. Right?"

I nodded. Swallowed.

"That's good. And the rest is just a matter of paper-work. And once that's over...."

That fork of purple streaked through his irises again and I was lost, captivated.

"Game on," Axel whispered.

CHAPTER 16

DONNA

B ella came to get me while I was still rehashing my conversation with Axel. Game on, he'd said. As though my official divorce would mark the beginning of something, not just the end of my marriage.

"Hey." My sister slid a book down in front of me, breaking me out of my trance. "I thought you could use a refresher on energy and element basics."

I stared down at the cracked leather cover of the Sanders's Grimoire. It smelled as it always had, of dust and dried herbs and old paper. I smiled as I ran my hand over the crystal-encrusted cover. "I haven't thought about this in years."

The oldest entries were courtesy of our ancestor, Edith Sanders. I flipped to the inside of the front cover where the family tree resided. Edith branched into her two daughters, Jasmine and Esmerelda. The line only followed the Sanders who remained at Storm Grove and raised their daughters in the craft. It stretched all the way down past Grand, and her twin sister Grace, to our mother Fiona, and her twin, Faelen, before dead-ending with us.

I traced the cursive letters that formed my sister's name. "Have you thought about names yet?"

Bella shook her head. "I'm a little afraid to, at least until I can get the demon situation handled."

I gave her a level look. "Do you really think you can control a demon? They were banished from the realm for causing chaos and destruction."

"Declan's not like that," she protested, once again leaping to that demon's defense.

I tapped the page with the family tree. "And what if you're wrong? This line might end with us."

"You think I don't know that?" she snapped. "You think that the stress of this whole situation doesn't keep me up at night?"

I put my hands out in a placating gesture. "Bella, I'm not attacking your choices. But what do you think Mom or Grand would say if they knew you were harboring a demon?"

She got to her feet. "I'm going for a walk."

"Bella," I called when she stood at the edge of the patio.

She stopped but didn't turn. "Mom and Grand didn't get everything right. They were witches but they were also human. They made plenty of mistakes. We all just do the best that we can for however long we can and hope like hell that it's enough."

I watched her disappear into the trees and then refocused on the family tree. My gaze flitted over the names that dead-ended. The twins who were born duds or had left and never returned to Shadow Cove, or hadn't carried on the family line with a set of twin girls. Bella's words echoed in my ears. She was right. The witches who'd come before had made mistakes. Grand had still been alive when Devon was born. Yet she hadn't recorded his birth because I'd had one boy instead of two girls.

What about the other bits we didn't bother to record? The marriages, and the other children all of whom were kin to the legacy witches. All of whom weren't important enough to mark the pages of this history. Hell, for all we knew, mom's sister, our Aunt Faelen was still alive and roaming the world oblivious to our existence.

I loved my son. I was proud of him and damn it, he deserved to show up in this book.

I dug through my purse until I found a pen. My hand-writing was nowhere near as neat as Edith's or Grand's or even Bella's but I was correcting this oversight.

I drew a line straight down from my name and beneath it I wrote, "Devon Eric Allen."

There. Take that Sanders legacy.

Feeling vindicated, I flipped to the pages at the back of the Grimoire, which were full of spells. Warding spells. Spells to create light or heat. Spells to make a witch invisible to her enemies. Had Bella cast that one to protect herself from the Bradburys? I would have to ask her.

An uneasy thought occurred. If the Bradburys found out that Bella was expecting a child that would be of their bloodline, would they try to sue for parental rights?

Or worse, would they try to kidnap my nieces after they were born?

I blew out a breath and got to my feet. I needed to talk to Bella. Nothing would get solved with me sitting on my ass with no one to answer my questions.

I was about to shut the book when an entry I hadn't seen before caught my eye. *Siphoning magic.*

My lips parted. It was in my mother's handwriting, which explained why I'd overlooked it. Her cursive was heavy on the loops and sometimes hard to read. If Declan hadn't told me about siphons I would have skimmed right by it.

Siphoning should only be done in a time of great need to protect yourself or your family as it will greatly deplete the magical practitioner you are pulling life force from. Irreparable brain damage has occurred and some who have been siphoned never recover.

I shivered at the warning. Stealing soul magic was seriously dark stuff, which Mom's warning reflected. But the demon had made it sound like siphoners were everywhere, lurking under every rhododendron. Waiting for the chance to bleed us dry.

It's best to have the cooperation of the one you are siphoning. If that is not possible, then have a partner help subdue the individual you plan to siphon as the spell can be draining. A tonic or potion might also be utilized.

"Oh, goddess," I breathed. Bella had said Zeke Bradbury had slipped her something. And his cousin drove the car. Two warlocks from a rival family. Had the attack which resulted in Bella's pregnancy been a botched attempt to steal her powers?

I slammed the book shut and then stuffed it into my oversized purse. I needed to find her, to ask if she had felt any of the symptoms. Because if the Bradburys had wanted to steal Bella's magic and hadn't been able to... they might try again.

I'd only taken two steps when the wards around the property started wailing an alert.

"Bella!" I took off running, heading for the portal, knowing that was exactly where my sister would go, to the heart of Storm Grove.

<hr>

Bella

"WE NEED A DUNGEON," I said to Kendra as I looked down at yet another wraith-riddled man who'd been making his way to the portal. "We don't have anywhere to keep these bastards."

There had been three more incursions while I was gone yesterday. The werewolves had subdued them all, but the pack was growing weary. Even with Donna and Axel's help, the danger of a breach was growing more serious by the hour.

"Someone wants that portal open, badly." Kendra agreed.

We didn't have a lot of options. If I killed the body holding the wraith, the wraith would be free to find another vessel and try again. It was like playing whack-a-mole with beings that needed no rest or food to keep going. They would never stop.

A moment later I spotted my sister running for all she was worth coming down the path. "Are you all right?"

I nodded and then turned to face Kendra. "Stuff this one in the broom closet in the bunkhouse for now. We'll figure out what to do with them later."

Kendra hauled the unconscious man to her feet but then Donna stepped forward, a frown on her face. "Wait. I think I know him."

"You do? How?"

"He works in the same office building as Lewis. His son played soccer on the team with Devon."

I flipped open the wallet. Current Florida driver's license. "Kendra, call Axel and have him run a check on this name on social media. Have him look up the address on Google, too. Then get yourself some sleep."

"What are you thinking?" The werewolf asked.

"I think this is a phony ID. And I think that whoever is sending the wraiths after the portal wants to keep us chasing our tails, so to speak, so we don't look closer to home."

Kendra moved off to the side and Donna knelt beside the unconscious man. "He's a good guy. Always donated money for the kid's uniforms. And after his wife died, he had three kids to raise."

A lump formed in my throat. It was easier to kill the wraith-ridden when I thought they were villains. The one who'd attacked Joseline had been for sure. But what about the one who Donna and I had served flambe over the portal? Had he been a good man who had slept with his body reflected in a mirror and been taken over when his guard was down?

I thought about Declan's words. *"It...affected me strangely and I find myself reluctant to leave you now that I know you can be so vulnerable."*

Because evil exploited vulnerability. Weaponized it. Goddess help me, but the demon I'd summoned wanted to protect me.

"I need to call the demon back," I said to my sister.

I expected her to protest but when she didn't right away I knew something was wrong.

"What is it?"

Her teeth sank into her lower lip and then she reached into her crossbody bag and extracted the grimoire. I took it when she handed it over and followed her finger when she pointed to the entry in mom's handwriting.

"Willingly be siphoned?" I frowned. "Why would anyone volunteer to have their magic stolen?"

"Bella, the other day, when I was hurt. You took my hand to create that fire."

"That's right," I said slowly.

"You were using my magic. Not against me, but to feed the witch-born fire. I didn't realize it at the time."

I folded my arms over my chest. "So, what are you saying? That I was siphoning from you?"

She shrugged. "I don't know. I was tired after I got back to the manor. I thought that was just because of the healing, but what if that's how siphoning works?"

"Donna, why are we talking about siphoning?" I

asked. "We have this wraith invasion to deal with and—"

She gripped my arm, her fingernails leaving little crescents in my skin. "Because. I think it's much more common than we knew. I think, Bella, I think that was what Zeke and his cousin wanted from you. And when they couldn't get it—"

"They raped me." The grimoire hit the ground at my feet and I would have gone down after it if my sister hadn't been holding me upright.

"I think you're going to have to follow through with your demon," she whispered.

"No," I croaked, my voice hoarse.

"Bells—"

"Donna, no. As in hell no. I will not promise that demon a baby."

She stroked my hair gently. "Weren't you just telling me that you think he didn't mean it?"

Yes, but it was one thing to think about it and maybe want to believe. Another entirely to risk one of my unborn children on the long shot.

I turned and stared up at my sister. "We can do it."

"What?" Donna stared at me, blank-faced.

"We can take the Bradburys out. Siphon them before they have a chance to siphon us."

Donna shifted, clearly uneasy with the suggestion. "You're talking about incapacitating an entire legacy family."

Deep in my womb, I felt a small flutter as one of my precious ones kicked and squirmed. I would eradicate the Bradburys if I had to but... "Just Zeke and his cousin.

As a warning shot. Then we dump them on the matri-arch's doorstep as an object lesson of what happens when you fuck with the Sanders sisters."

Our gazes locked and then Donna nodded slowly. "Okay. What do we need to do?"

CHAPTER 17

DONNA

"No." I shook my head at Bella. "Absolutely not."

"Come on, Don." Axel stood between us, the dumbass willing participant in what I was sure would result in a massive clusterfuck. "It's part of my job to help Bells out with stuff like this."

I pinched the bridge of my nose. I'd been regretting saying yes out by the portal ever since we got back and my sister had morphed into a mad scientist on a mission. She'd looked so desperate at that moment that even though my gut churned madly, I'd agreed. Bella needed to do something to take her power back from the Bradburys. Something that didn't involve the demon. But if I had known what she planned....

Actually, *plan* was too generous a word for this kerfuffle. "It is not part of your job to be a damn guinea pig, Axel. We don't know what this potion will do to you, never mind the siphon spell."

Bella pulled the grimoire closer and tapped it with a

fingernail. "It says right here that a willing source is best."

"But we don't even know if Axel has witch blood. The spell could have unintended consequences." Horrible visions of Axel writhing in pain at our feet filled my head. Or worse. Staring sightlessly up at the two of us as his heart beat its last. "Maybe I can try it."

But Bella was shaking her head. "No, you need to practice the siphoning spell and you can't do that if you're drained."

Axel gripped my hand. "Don, it's okay. Really. I'd rather take the risk than send the two of you out there with a potion that might fail and an untried spell that could blow up in your faces."

"We're doing this, with or without you," Bella's chin went up. She had a smudge of charcoal on her cheek and her white maternity dress was smeared with the stuff as she'd had to filter the sleepytime tonic for impurities to make sure it would be magically undetectable.

I stared at the vial of clear liquid. It had no scent and if I didn't know better, I'd say it was water.

Unfortunately, I knew better.

Axel gave my hand one more squeeze and then let go. I held my breath as he reached for the vial. "All of it?"

"Yeah," Bella nodded.

He brought the vial to his lips. Without considering what I was doing I lunged forward before he could knock it back and stayed his hand.

His gray gaze met mine and held.

"Bella. Give us a minute here," I whispered.

Even pregnant my sister could move silently when

she wanted. I felt my awareness of her fade a moment before the door scraped along the floor, shutting us in the den alone.

"I don't want you to do this," I said to Axel.

He searched my features. "Why not?"

How could I explain all the feelings that haunted me the way Annabeth haunted Storm Grove?

"I know that we just met and that we don't know each other all that well," I began, my gaze locked on the floor between us. "And these feelings are just...they don't make any sense."

"Don, look at me." He cupped my face, holding me still so I met his gaze. And I had no choice but to admit the truth.

"I need you." The words escaped as if they were making a jailbreak.

My admission shocked me to my core. I had never said those words to anyone. Not even Bella. I was a strong, independent woman who had been wrestling my wonky brain for her entire life. I'd established a business, raised a son, kept calm, and carried on all by my lonesome. Even when I felt defective or broken or worn down to a nub I'd been standing on my own. I'd always thought admitting that I couldn't go it alone was a sign of weakness. But I didn't feel weak. Vulnerable, yes, because now he could use that information against me. Even so, I kept speaking.

"These last few days, with Bella, my husband, the wraiths, demons, and werewolves...it would have been too much for me to handle. I would have shut down. Turned my back on all of it out of self-preservation. I've done it before. It would have been too much for me to handle if not for you. But you've been giving me this quiet support. Helping me so I could help others. Propping me up so I could do what needed to be done. So I could be present. You just shouldered some of the weight that would have broken me."

Tears were spilling over my lids as fear took center stage. I hadn't known what was missing. And now I couldn't imagine going on without it.

His expression was still. He hadn't made a noise. In fact, I wasn't even sure he was still breathing. Fuck it, I was going to say it all because who knew if I'd get another chance?

"I need you because I can't afford to shut down. Bella needs me to be here for her and her babies. And I want to be here for her. Without you, I'll crack and crumble. Please, don't make me do this alone."

"Don," he whispered. And then his lips were on mine.

I hadn't lost myself in the first kiss because my mind had been on Lewis and my neighbors. The second had caught me off guard. But this one....

Pure. Perfect. Everything that a kiss ought to be.

I never would have come up for air. Would have happily drowned in him. But he stepped back, out of reach, and then knocked back the vial.

"I'm not going anywhere, Don," He vowed and then collapsed onto the floor.

"Bella!" I shrieked.

198

Bella

"WHAT DO YOU MEAN DECLAN LEFT?" I asked Annabeth.

The ghost made a palms-up gesture. "Exactly that. His wards are down and there is no stink of demon outside his room. Now, my toll."

I'd stuck my athame in my pocket and withdrew it. Was about to prick my finger and give the ghost her payment when I heard Donna shriek my name.

"Shit," I barreled through the apparition and pushed open the study doors. Axel was sprawled on the oriental rug, the vial with the sleepytime potion empty. Donna knelt beside his limp form. Her hands fluttered over the top of him like moths unable to settle.

"Does he have a pulse?" I asked, reaching for his neck. Blood rushed beneath his warm skin, strong and steady.

"My payment, witch," Annabeth said from behind me.

"Not now," I hissed and reached for the grimoire. "Donna, we need to do this, now."

"I can't..." My sister's eyes were red-rimmed. I'd never seen her so overcome, not even at Grand's funeral. She was the strong one.

I gripped her by the shoulders. "Listen to me. You can and you will. He wants you to be prepared. That's why he volunteered."

Silent tears tracked down her face.

"My payment, witch," Annabeth shrieked.

Fucking diva. "Fine," I bitched but before I could prick my finger Donna snatched the blade from me.

"You want blood?" She drew the blade over her palm. "I hope you fucking choke on it."

"Donna, no!" I shouted. "That's too much!"

But it was too late. Annabeth had latched onto Donna's hand and drank greedily. Her figure grew more solid with every swallow, the colors more vivid. Donna's tears had dried. An ethereal wind straight from the soul plane blew through the manor as she ripped her hand free of Annabeth's and reached for me.

Annabeth stumbled back, her ridiculous gown causing her to trip and land on her backside. I saw the phantom stare at her hands in awe. A chilling expression of avarice crossed her face as she rounded to where I was crouched over Axel.

"Back off," Donna snarled the command and it echoed with distant thunder. I could feel her power. It raised all the hairs on my arms.

And Annabeth....

Murderer. She'd killed her sister. And their infants she'd sacrificed... I could see it all, the lust, the greed, the fear of death. Rotten, she was evil incarnate, had struck a deal with dark forces so she could remain here. Could continue to prey on the weak.

Annabeth's gaze snapped to me and fear gripped her. I knew and she knew that I knew. I felt sick because I'd been feeding her, using her like I didn't have a tiger by the tail all this time.

Donna thrust one hand out as though she was doing something to ward off the phantom. The other hand, the one she had cut, was stretched out behind her, as though grasping for something.

Me. And in a flash, I knew what she was doing. I took her hand and felt the connection as magic flowed between us. She pulled, I pushed, and then we stood shoulder to shoulder. I held the grimoire so she could see the spell.

Wind from the North
Wild and free
Siphon her power
So mote it be.

We repeated the chant three times. Annabeth screamed. The sound curdled my blood and raised every hair on my body. We stood transfixed as Annabeth began to crack, right up the middle and then a brilliant band of white emerged as though she'd been carved by a sunbeam.

"Keep going," Donna snapped.

We said the chant a fourth time. A fifth. More cracks appeared. On the sixth, Annabeth's eyes blazed with red fire.

"Holy shit," I breathed. "She's a wraith."

How had she hidden her true nature from us all this time? Could all wraiths take blood tolls to become corporeal? Or was it just because Annabeth had been a witch?

"Again," Donna snapped. "Let's finish this."

I followed her lead and as the final word for the seventh chant fell from our lips I felt a flood of power hit me like a wave on the shore. It crested and broke, the light blinding. I shut my eyes and turned away to shield my gaze.

The power washed over the three of us and settled in all the low spots, just like water in dimples of sand. Trickled down and in and when it finally faded...

"Annabeth?"

There was nothing but a pile of ash where the phantom had been.

Donna's bloody hand covered her mouth. "We killed her. We killed a wraith."

"That's not possible." No power could kill a wraith because they were already dead. That was an undisputed fact. And we had just drained every drop of whatever it was that held Annabeth together for all these years and absorbed it in full.

"Axel." Donna got on her hands and knees beside him. "Oh goddess, he took some of that in."

"We need to wake him up."

"How?" Donna asked but I was already at the work table, hunting for the jar of smelling salts. I found it and unstoppered it, taking a whiff to make sure I had the right vile. The sting of ammonia burned my sinuses and I fought the urge to hurl. I handed it to Donna. "Hold this under his nose."

She did as I said. Two breaths later, Axel was coughing and knocking Donna's hand away.

Donna's shoulders sagged. "He's all right."

I took the vile from her and then sank onto the stool by the workbench. "You were right, Donna."

She was too busy helping Axel sit up to pay any attention to me.

"It's okay, Don," he slurred. And when his eyes opened....

"Oh, my goddess." Tongues of lightning forked through his gray irises causing all my hackles to rise. "Axel, I know what you are."

Donna

"W<small>HAT</small>?" I asked. "How?"

"His eyes. Only one being can contain electricity that way. He's a fury," Bella looked as though Axel had transformed into a venomous spider. I didn't miss the way she moved to put the worktable between herself and her assistant.

"A fury?" I looked back to Axel. "Like from Greek myths?"

"They aren't myths," my sister said. "Though they haven't been seen on this plane for hundreds of years."

Axel looked from me to Bella. His brows pulled together and I knew he had picked up on Bella's fear. "What's a fury?"

"Depends on which story you read," I told him. "Gods, demons, demigods of vengeance or justice. Born out of blood and seafoam. Basically, badass creatures with which one did not fuck unless they had a death wish."

Every muscle in his body was tense. "Bells, I won't hurt you."

She nodded a little too quickly. "I know."

He looked back at me, those eerie irises flickering with a warning of the power that lay within.

A power we had just enhanced with a blooded wraith's soul.

"It's probably a good thing we didn't try to siphon you," I winked at him. "We probably couldn't have handled what you've got going on."

He relaxed and the tension in the room lessened.

"How are you feeling?" I asked him because damn her, Bella still wasn't saying anything. "Any aftereffects from the sleepytime tonic?"

He reached up and rubbed the back of his neck. "Just a little cottonmouth and a mild headache. I'll live."

Again his gaze held mine and I smiled. "I'm relieved to hear it."

I helped him to his feet and he stared for a long moment at the pile of ash that had been Annabeth. The lightning in his eyes grew in intensity. "She killed her twin."

I jerked. "What?"

"That's how she stayed here. Sacrificed her twin and buried the body on the property. It tethered her to this plane." His hands clenched. "You gave her comeuppance, Don."

There was a sepulchral note of finality in his voice that I'd never heard before. As if he were passing judgment.

Bella flinched but nodded. "He's right. I saw it in her before we...did what we did."

Axel shut his eyes. "I think I should go lie down. My headache is getting worse."

"Want me to get you anything?" I asked.

He smiled down at me. "No, Don. I'll be all right."

I wasn't so sure but didn't protest. He probably needed to process what had happened. I did, too.

After Axel shut the door behind him, Bella sagged like a puppet whose strings had been cut.

"What's your problem?" I snapped. "He's still the same sweet guy he was this morning."

"That's just it," Bella said. "It shouldn't be possible for Axel to be what he is. Furies were always female."

I stared at her. "But you said—"

"The boys were killed at birth," my sister whispered, her gaze glued to the door "Because sooner or later they always went mad."

CHAPTER 18

BELLA

After what Donna had done, killing the unkillable, and the revelation that Axel was a freaking fury, scrying for the Bradburys was a welcome distraction.

At least for me.

Zeke was at the family's stronghold. His cousin, the one whose name I didn't know, was out on Shadow Lake. Unless he was in the middle of a corporate picnic, he would be the easier of the two to isolate and siphon.

Donna stared out the window of my DeVille, her expression blank.

"I still can't believe that Annabeth was a wraith," I said. "I was feeding my blood to a wraith."

No response.

"Come on, Donna. Aren't you going to yell at me? Tell me I'm an idiot for using her?"

She looked over at me with a small smile. "You did what you had to do."

I blew out a breath. "We don't need to do this right now if you're not up to it."

"I'm fine," she said in that same dead voice.

"Is it about Axel," I whispered. "I know you like him."

"I'm still married," she murmured.

"Right, married, not dead."

She flinched and I felt like a jackass. "What I mean is, that you have developed perfectly natural feelings for a man who has treated you with consideration and respect."

"Bella," she said and I could feel her eyes on me. "Do you want to talk to me about your highly inappropriate fascination for that demon you summoned?"

"No," I breathed.

"Then do me a favor and shut the hell up." She turned back to the window.

I bristled but clamped my lips together. Fair enough.

Shadow Lake had been formed when the river had been damned up at the turn of the last century. The town of Shadow Cove sat on the western side, opposite Declan's hotel. Private homes dotted most of the southern shoreline. But the northernmost part backed up to National Park land. That was our destination, according to the scrying crystal.

I went over the inventory for our mission. The sleepy time tonic had been added to a flask. To get close enough to slip it to our target, Donna had agreed to wear a glamour spell so she wouldn't be recognized by any stray magic users. The spell made her nose longer and her build taller than it normally was as well as adding the illusion of long blond hair. She was wearing another of the outfits I'd bought for her, a pair of plum slacks and a black shell. The final touch was the pair of oversized sunglasses.

I parked in one of the parking areas behind the boat launch, making sure the highly recognizable DeVille was hidden. For my own disguise, I wore a scarf over my hair and another pair of sunglasses as well as a blue maternity shirt and pants. Not many people around Shadow Cove knew about the pregnancy. Combined with the fact that I wasn't the kind of witch who went to public beaches regularly, I felt sure I wouldn't be recognized.

The sun was low on the horizon when we got out of the car. I froze when I recognized the battered Ford Focus I'd climbed into the night I'd been attacked. "That's it. That's his car."

Donna nodded and walked right up to the driver's side like she had every right. Her hand closed over the handle and she tried it. "Unlocked. You can tell this guy lives out in the boonies."

Either that or being a Bradbury gave him a sense of security. Maybe he couldn't imagine that anyone would come after him.

Donna was busy rooting through the glovebox. She came up with a crumpled vehicle registration card. "Nelson T. Bradbury the third," she read.

"I didn't want to know that."

She stared up at me. "Are you sure you want to go through with this?"

"Positive," I nodded even though I felt as though I'd swallowed a salamander that was wriggling its way through my insides.

Nelson and Zeke. Zeke or Nelson. One of them had fathered my children. Both posed a risk to me, to my sister, and, eventually, to my girls. For a moment the image of Annabeth fracturing with cracks of light flashed before my eyes. But no, that wouldn't happen to a living person. We were just going to disempower him. Siphon off his magic. Maybe damage his brain. No biggie.

"Bella, you're staggering like a drunk." Donna caught me by the arm and guided me to a picnic table. "Sit down here and let me do a quick survey of the area."

"Be careful," I said and felt somewhat reassured when she squeezed my hand.

My big sister. Older by all of four minutes. And she'd always acted as though the weight of the world rested on her shoulders. Even though I'd come into my magic early, it was clear that she was the stronger witch. The stronger sister.

She'd neutralized a wraith. I still couldn't get my head around that fact. It filled me with elation. If she could destroy a being as powerful as Annabeth could she do it again? Maybe even without killing the host in the process? The war without an end might have an end in sight after all.

"I think I found him," Donna said as she reappeared by my side. "Over by the dock. He's fishing."

"What's our play?" I asked.

"DID?" She raised a brow. "Will it work?"

DID stood for damsel in distress. I shrugged. "I never did a reflection on him. But based on what I know, he'll come with you because you look helpless. Especially in that getup."

"Bait for a predator." She smiled grimly. "All right. I'll try and lure him into that grove over there. Be ready. As soon as he takes a drink, you need to pounce."

I reached out and grabbed her hand. "In case I haven't already said this, thank you. For having my back."

Donna squeezed my hand. "Don't worry, sis. I'll always have your back."

Donna

"Excuse me, sir?" I added extra honey to my slight southern accent, though I hadn't thought about it beforehand. Maybe because I was in disguise.

Nelson, or the man who I thought was Nelson, turned to face me. He was shorter than my enhanced five foot nine by several inches and had a wide space between his two front teeth.

"What you want?" he asked and spat tobacco as he eyed my breasts.

To punch you in the nose. I thought and the image of doing just that brought a genuine smile to my face. "I was hoping you could help me. I've lost my little dog in the trees over there." I pointed to the spot where Bella was hopefully lying in wait.

"She's only ten pounds and afraid of her own shadow," I added. "Please."

I could tell he wanted to refuse. The inbred stain

obviously wasn't an animal lover. But I upped the ante by pulling out my wallet.

"I'll pay you. Let's see. I have two hundred and twenty-five dollars." I looked up from riffling through imaginary bills. "Please. You can have it all. I just want to get my Mitzy back."

He spat again and then laid down his fishing pole, beady little eyes bright with avarice. "All right then, Ms... what you say your name was?"

"Muffy." Goddess, I was a horrible liar. Mitzy and Muffy. Ugh.

"I'll be glad to help you out, Muffy," Nelson said and then patted me on the butt.

It wasn't every day I found a man who made Lewis look like a halfway decent human being, but Nelson was giving it the ol' college try. At least the letch was following me toward the trees, away from the eyes of the other people who were enjoying the public beach.

When we were just inside the tree line I fished a flask out of my purse and pretended to take a drink, making sure I kept my lips compressed so that none of the potion entered my system. I had the jar of smelling salts just in case, but using them would end the ruse too soon.

"Whatchya got there, Muffy?" Nelson gripped me by the arm hard enough to leave a bruise.

"Just a little bit of whiskey," I said. "It helps calm my nerves. You want some?"

I held out the flask and tried not to look anxious. We could probably do the spell without having Nelson knocked out but not without him drawing attention to what was going on. And if he got away before we siphoned him he'd be on his guard.

Nelson took the flask and tipped it up. He made a face. "This don't taste like nothin'."

Then his eyes rolled back in his head.

Bella stepped out from where she'd been hiding behind a large boulder. "Goddess, I hope he isn't the father. What an idiot."

Her words were bold but I could see the tightness of her jaw.

I went to her and took her hand. "Okay, just like we did before. Seven times in a row."

Wind from the North
Wild and free
Siphon his power
So mote it be.

WE CHANTED the siphoning spell over and over with no interruption. The energy that flowed between our clasped hands was different. Less desperation on my part, more determination on Bella's. This mattered to her. It mattered to me because this man had hurt my sister. He'd shattered her confidence, her trust in herself and in those around her. I think before her attack, Bella had truly believed that all the evil in the world came from wraiths and demons. Not shitheels like Nelson or even emotionally abusive dicks like

Lewis. Those who built themselves up by tearing others down.

The white glow surrounded Nelson and then came the wave. It was nowhere near as powerful as it had been with Annabeth. I'd been braced for it, expecting the energy to feel as dirty as the previous owner. But it was raw power there for the taking.

"Is he still alive?" Bella asked.

I didn't want to touch him to check. Luckily, Nelson let out a loud snore at that moment.

"Bright side? If he is brain damaged, I doubt anyone will notice." I reached out for her hand and squeezed. "You good?"

She nodded and smiled. "Yeah. I think I am."

Hand in hand we walked away from the snoring Bradbury.

"I still think you should report him," I said to Bella. "He doesn't pose a risk to the mortal authorities now. And he could still hurt someone else."

"After we take care of Zeke." She squeezed my hand tightly. "Once that's done we can talk about the next step."

I leaned against the car and removed the glamour charm while Bella worked her magic with the scrying crystal. I was tired and wanted to call it a day. "Hey Bells, do you think—"

"It's not working," Bella looked up from the map. "I'm not getting a hit on Zeke."

I didn't know much about scrying, other than I'd never been able to do it because it required both focus and magic. "Maybe you're just tired."

"I had him earlier," she said.

"Looking for something, witchling?"

We both jumped at the sound of Declan's voice. "Where the hell did you come from?" I asked.

"Answer's in the question," he murmured, his eyes not leaving Bella's face.

She'd gone pale and her lips were parted. "You can't have killed him. I ordered you not to kill him."

"And you're going to rescind that order," Declan said. "And let me kill him as we originally discussed."

"No," Bella covered her stomach with both hands "No, I won't."

"Then you won't get the warlock." The demon shrugged. "I can move him from place to place for the rest of eternity if need be."

"You wouldn't dare," Bella's eyes were huge.

"Oh, witchling. Don't tell me what I would or would not dare."

"Az—" she began but the demon vanished before she got the word out.

"What now?" I asked her.

She shook her head. "Damned if I know."

"Move over," I nudged her. "I'm driving."

Bella

THAT SNEAKY DEMON. A day ago I would have called his bluff. If he kept Zeke far away from me, he could play hide the warlock until the end of time. But after magically castrating Nelson I'd felt as though I'd found some-thing I'd lost. Something necessary to my survival. And I feared that I'd never be whole again unless I siphoned Zeke.

"He has to want something else," Donna was saying as she headed back to Storm Grove. "Not just one of your babies. We need to find out whatever it is Declan wants most and use that as your leverage."

"Leverage," I repeated the word and shook my head. "There's no such thing when it comes to demons."

She cut me a sideways glance. "Yesterday you thought there was no way to kill a wraith. But we did it."

"This is different," I protested. "Declan is old. Very old. He does what he wants when he wants because that's what demons do."

"But what does he want?" Donna insisted as she took the turns heading back to the manor.

"I don't know," I growled. "It's all just guessing at this point."

"Look I know you're frustrated—"

"Frustrated?" I spat. "Are you even kidding me right now?

"What?" She looked at me, eyes wide.

"Pull over."

She must have thought I was going to be sick because she stopped the car in the middle of the road. "Bella, what is it?"

I shoved the heavy door open and got out. "What isn't it? My house is a mess, and my PA—who I haven't paid in months—is a fucking male fury. A demon is holding my rapist hostage! I've got wraiths making constant runs for the portal and to top it off I can't do this!"

Donna was still seated in the car. "Can't do what?"

I gestured to my baby bump. "Be a mother! Protect my girls. I've endangered them before they're even born. Donna, I don't know what the hell I'm doing! I'm doing everything wrong." The last word came out as a choked gasp.

Donna got out of the car and came to where I stood. "It's okay, Bella."

I made a horrible gargling noise as my throat cinched up like a drawstring purse. It wasn't all right. Didn't she understand? There was a sharp pain in my chest and I couldn't breathe.

My sister guided me to the open car and gestured for me to have a seat. When I did, she crouched in front of me and held my hands. "You're overwhelmed right now,"

I looked at her as tears tracked down my face.

"I've been there," Donna soothed, her voice steady and strong. "The other day. I got lost in town. You know what helped pull me out of it? Axel."

My eyebrows drew together. Listening to her words kept me from wheezing for breath.

Her clear green eyes were steady. "He showed up for me. I never knew how badly I needed that. Just someone to show up for me. And I think you need the same thing."

I clutched her hands tightly. She smiled. "Don't worry. You've got me. We're part of each other, remember? What happens to you happens to me. And I will defend these babies with my life. Even from you if I must."

Her words helped me draw a deep breath. Then another. I managed to croak, "Really?"

"Cross my heart and hope to die." She made a gesture I hadn't seen since we were little. "You believe me, right?"

At my nod, her shoulders relaxed. "Okay, good. Now, I need to bring you home to rest."

I swung my legs around and into the car. "Where are you going?"

She paused in the middle of walking through the headlight beams. "To negotiate with a demon."

CHAPTER 19

DONNA

I'd once had a hyper focused period when I'd decided to learn about battle strategy. I'd devoured books on military tactics, read about sieges in countries that I'd never heard of, and the wins and losses of long-dead civilizations. After research burnout had set in, and I'd been recovering from an information hangover, I'd decided that had been the most pointless obsession of my life.

Until my sister and I were stuck between a demon and a hard place.

While Bella had been struggling with her hormones and overwhelm, my wonky brain had been chewing on the problem. And the problem, at least the way I saw it, was Declan. The demon was the wild card in the mix. His powers couldn't be contained by witches, not even witches riding high on siphoned magic. He was the oncoming general with an endless arsenal and he would be relentless in pursuit of his goal. If we didn't give the demon what he wanted, he would find someone else to take hostage.

Joseline, maybe. Or Axel. Or my son, Devon.

I was the citadel commander of the city under attack. I held the defensive position. My resources were limited. My best and only option would be to negotiate a truce and make sure he didn't lay waste to the city.

Because it was better to have the stronger force by your side to protect from the next incursion.

After dropping Bella at home, I checked on Axel. He lay on his back, a book lying open on his chest. His complexion looked pale under his tan.

I picked up the book and read the title. Monsters and myths of the ancient world. Poor Axel. He was desperate for answers. I didn't know if I should tell him what Bella told me, that all male furies went insane and they were killed at birth because of it. Would that trigger a self-fulfilling prophecy?

A problem for another day. At the moment sleep was the best thing for him. Joseline had come out of my room in human form as I shut his door.

"Hey you," I said to the werewolf girl. "I need to go out for a while. Do you think you can do something for me?"

When she nodded I brought her down to the entry and showed her the incantation that Edith Sanders had carved into the lintel above the front door when Storm Grove had first been constructed.

"As soon as I'm outside I want you to say these words. It'll keep the house and everyone inside locked behind a shield."

Joseline stared at me with wide dark eyes. "How will you get back in?"

"I won't. Not until you let me in. Just say the spell backward, from the last line to the first and the charm will dissolve." At her worried look, I added. "It's just a precaution. I need to know that you and Axel and Bella and her babies are all safe."

I could have asked Bella to do this, but my sister was already on emotional overload and I was worried about the health of my nieces. Joseline would do as I said without argument.

When she nodded, I squeezed her shoulder. "Maybe I'll pick up a pizza on my way back and we can watch a movie. Pick one out for us on my computer, okay?"

She nodded and I kissed the top of her head then headed out the door.

At the bottom of the steps, I turned to face the house and waited. The spell had only been enacted once, to my knowledge. When I was very young, maybe three or four. Grand had been away and Mom had sensed something in the woods. Bella and I couldn't see what happened on the outside so curiosity compelled me to watch.

Magic prickled in the air and made all the small hairs rise on my arms. The wind from the soul plane blew. And then, to my left came a great scraping sound, like stone being dragged across stone.

"Well, I'll be." A gravelly voice with a Cockney accent said. "If it ain't little Donna, all growed up."

I blinked because there was no way I was seeing what I was seeing. But yes, the gargoyle really was talking to me.

"What's a matter, luv?" The other gargoyle spoke with a similar accent, though the voice was much higher pitched. "Cat got your tongue?"

"No," I said and then stared at the two carved creatures in awe. "Clyde? Hyde? Is that really you?"

"In the flesh," Clyde said and then his carved eyebrows pulled closer together between his horns. "Though I don't reckon the missus appreciates the name you gave her."

The missus? "Oh sorry, my bad. I was little when I named you. I never thought..." What? That they could hear me? Or that one might be female?

The gargoyle with the higher-pitched voice folded her arms across her chest. "Well, no time like the present."

"Oh, you want a new name?" My head was spinning but one name surfaced. I internally winced as I offered, "How about Bonnie?"

"There, luv. That's downright pretty that is." Clyde sounded like the father from *My Fair Lady*. Maybe I should have gone with Eliza instead.

The female gargoyle nodded and then stretched out her wings. "It'll do. Go on about your business, little miss. We've got the watch."

"Okay," I said, and then turned and headed to my car. Gargoyles come to life. And why not? Axel was a fury, and the stone statues I'd been talking to since I was knee-high to a grasshopper were guarding Storm Grove Manor while I went off to negotiate with a demon.

Hard to believe that a fistful of days ago I was helping

my son unpack his dorm room. That Donna Sanders-Allen seemed like an entirely different person.

Bella called me while I was en route to the demon's hotel. I hit the button on the dash and her voice filtered through the speakers. "Are you sure this is a good idea?"

"If he wanted to hurt me he would have done it the other day when he had the chance. You told me yourself that he hasn't killed anyone. So why would he start with me?"

My bravado was entirely false. I was banking on the fact that the demon wanted something from my sister, something other than a baby.

"I should be with you," Bella said.

"No, you absolutely should not," I spoke with conviction. "Who knows what all this siphoned magic is doing to the twins? You need to rest."

Besides, whatever was going on between my sister and the demon would only complicate matters.

The demon met me on the steps, almost as if he'd known I was coming. He looked the same as he had every time I'd met him. Normal. Every hair was in place and not the slightest bit demonic.

But I'd smelled the brimstone. I'd seen him reflect Bella's magic back at her. Seen him vanish in a puff of smoke. Looks could be deceiving.

"Ms. Sanders-Allen." He held the door to my car. "Where is your charming sister?"

"Recovering." I watched his face carefully. Was that a flash of regret in his dark eyes? "All this stress isn't good for her or the babies."

He swallowed and then gestured to the hotel. "I've reserved the conference room for us."

"Lead the way," I murmured and was surprised when he put a hand on the small of my back to usher me forward. It was a courteous old-world sort of gesture. Not something that I would have expected from a demon.

Then again, was Declan even still a demon? His scent was changing, diminishing from how strong it had been. He picked a gender and was trying to fit into the human world. He hadn't killed anyone, hadn't attacked us, not even with wraiths.

The silver lining to my wonky brain? I saw connections that others missed. And my brain was busy fitting the pieces of this demon together, trying to see the whole picture.

I studied him as we walked, my heart pounding. Maybe I was way off base, but there was a time when all I'd known was Storm Grove and the supernatural world. I hadn't fit in there and had gone off to college and realized there were many other ways to live other than as a legacy witch. I'd walked away. Formed a new life.

What if... what if the demon my sister summoned didn't *want* to be a demon anymore? What if he just didn't know any better way to exist?

It was a long shot and I was no gambler. But it made as much sense as anything else.

The conference room was a vision of old-world elegance meeting modern comfort. A conference table that could seat twelve dominated the space and the chairs were heavily upholstered in a paisley fabric that went with the curtains and rug. The floor-to-ceiling windows gleamed under the dimmed recess lighting. Outside I could see the burbling two-tiered fountain lit with solar lights.

The demon held out a chair for me and I sat.

"Can I get you anything?" Declan raised a brow and I shook my head.

"No, I have a pizza date with my werewolf girl after we're done here," I replied and then gestured around the room. "Did you decorate this space? It's very elegant."

A genuine smile stole across his face. It was very different than the smug smirk he typically wore. "I did. And I take that as a compliment considering your background in design."

"I wouldn't change a thing," I assured him. "Except for the circumstances that bring us here. We don't want to be your enemies, Declan."

He lifted his chin. "I'm a demon. The world is always my enemy."

"You were telling me about demons the other day. Things that Bella and I had never heard. And we're legacy witches." I folded my hands and leaned forward. "If we weren't taught the truth about your kind, then no one on this plane knows. Except for you."

His dark gaze studied my face for a long moment. "What is it you are proposing Donna Sanders-Allen?"

"A truce. Trade of information. You teach us about demons and in exchange, we'll do our best to give you human experiences."

His brows pulled down. "What makes you think I want that?"

I shrugged. "Call it woman's intuition."

He drummed his long fingertips on the conference table. "And the babes?"

"The babies are my sister's. She will die to protect them." I told him. "As much as she wants to siphon Zeke Bradbury's magic and as much as I want to see that rapist behind bars, we won't trade the next generation of Sanders witches for him or anyone else. Not now. Not ever."

Strong emotion flashed across Declan's face. It was like lightning striking. A blinding ribbon that was there and gone.

"You will swear to this, Donna Sanders-Allen?" Declan asked. "Make a blood vow?"

The intensity of his question startled me. A blood vow wasn't something a witch entered into lightly. Through magical compulsion, it could never be broken, as long as both parties lived. No do-overs and no takebacks.

What was it he wanted so badly? The vow that Bella and I would never give up the babies? But if that were the case, Declan would never fulfill the role he'd been summoned for...

The final puzzle piece snapped into place. "Oh, my goddess. That's what you want. For the stalemate to go on forever. Because if the purpose she summoned you for isn't fulfilled then you don't have to go back."

His throat bobbed. I hadn't known a demon could look vulnerable, but in that instant, Declan did.

I let out a long breath and nodded. "Okay, I think we

have something to build on here. Now it's just a matter of hashing through the details."

The demon snapped his fingers and a stack of papers and a knife appeared on the table between us. "As always, I'm way ahead of you."

Bella

I PACED the confines of my bedroom, listening as Donna read the demon's contract out loud over the speakerphone. My back ached and my head was pounding. "You're saying Azmodeous *doesn't* want one of my babies?"

Donna made a tsking sound. "No, he doesn't. He also doesn't want you to use that summoning name ever again. It's...rude to remind him where he came from and delays his transition to human."

I stopped and stared out the window. The pain in my back tightened and I blew out a breath.

"Bells?" Donna said. "This is as good as it's going to get for us. He can help us. The knowledge alone about demons and wraiths. We're better off having him as an ally than an enemy."

She wasn't wrong. "And he'll let us siphon Zeke's magic?"

"If that's what you want, then he'll agree to it. Reluctantly. He still wants to kill the Bradburys for touching you against your will." Donna lowered her voice. "I think he's developing feelings for you, Bells. And he doesn't know what to do with them because you're his summoner and potentially his jailer. He wants to include five dates with you in the contract."

Dating a demon. I began pacing again. It was either that or laugh hysterically.

"Listen, he'll help us with the portal attacks, even standing a shift. He does not want that portal open any more than we do. It's not gonna get better than this, sis."

I huffed out a breath and shut my eyes. Donna couldn't sign the contract lightly. Once she did, she would be compelled to see it through to the end. No alterations, no amendments once the document was signed. A blood oath was forever.

"Are you sure this is the best way?" I whispered.

"I really am," Donna murmured. "I know the temptation of giving in to impulses. But that's why Declan's here in the first place. That impulsiveness is going to get you or your children killed. Take it from your stick-in-the-mud sister. Make a plan and stick to it."

I squeezed my eyes shut. "Let me talk to him."

"Bells," Donna began.

"Now, Donna." I knew she was trying to protect me but there was only so much I would allow her to do.

I heard her say, "She wants to talk to you," and a moment later the demon came on the line.

"Problem, witchling?" he crooned.

"I don't want my sister to sign that contract." I turned in a circle, trying to ignore my growing discomfort. "If the contract is everything she says it is, I ought to be the one who signs it."

"Because you summoned me?" he asked.

"No." I breathed. "Because I owe it to her."

Donna had gone her whole life believing she was a dud. She didn't deserve to be tied to a contract for life. "The two of you come back here and—"

I gasped and doubled over as the backache spread to my midsection.

"Bella?" Declan's tone had sharpened. "What is it?"

My eyes opened and horror flooded me. "Oh, my goddess."

"Witchling!" Declan shouted. "What's wrong?"

I couldn't answer. My gaze was glued to the mirror where, instead of my reflection, I saw them.

Wraiths. Dozens of them fanning out like spokes on a wheel. And in the center...

The alarm for the wards sounded just as the pain in my back intensified.

"The portal is under attack," I gasped and gripped the phone tightly. "And I think I'm going into labor."

CHAPTER 20

DONNA

Something had changed. I could tell by the way Declan stood. Tension radiated from his every pore. What was Bella saying that had made him look like that?

"Bella?" He snapped and when he turned to me I saw flames leaping in his eyes. "I lost her."

"What's going on?" I asked as he thrust my phone back at me.

"Bella thinks she's going into labor. And she says wraiths are descending on the portal."

Had I heard that correctly? "Now?"

"No time," the demon snapped and then held out a hand.

I looked down at the contract. "We didn't sign—"

"Bella wants to do it." Declan gripped my hand and vanished the contract and blade. And then us.

It was an unnerving experience, traveling the way demons do. It felt as though my entire body came apart and then had to be pieced back together, one molecule at a time.

Declan released me and I went down on my hands and knees on the gravel drive of Storm Grove, doing my best not to retch as what little that had been in my stomach was sloshed around.

"Don!"

I looked up in time to see Axel struggling in the hold of the gargoyles. "Clyde, Bonnie, it's okay," I told them. "He's with us."

"If you say so, little miss." They dropped him and Axel landed in a crouch. He was a blur as he moved toward me and then I was in his arms.

"You okay?" he asked. "Joseline told me that you were going to negotiate with the demon."

I clutched him to me. "Yeah, I did."

"Where's Bella?" Declan demanded.

"Here." My sister leaned against the door frame, her face twisted in pain. "We need to get to the portal."

"You're in labor," I pulled away from Axel and moved to her side. "Bella, it isn't safe."

"It's my purpose," she gritted out and then squeezed her eyes shut.

Of all the crappy timing.... I blew out a breath. "Let me siphon your power."

That made her eyes open wide. "What?"

"I promise that if I don't die, I'll give them right back." I tried to smile but it felt forced. "You can't go into battle like this."

"She's right, witchling." The demon had come up to

Bella's other side. "It isn't safe, not with those kinds of numbers."

"I have Axel," I said. "I have the werewolves and the gargoyles. And if I can borrow your magic, I can get the job done in time to meet my new nieces."

"But," Bella protested and then bent low, blowing like a winded horse. "Who'll deliver the twins?"

"I will," the demon said.

We all stared at him.

"What? I'm thousands of years old. You think I can't catch a couple of newborns?"

Oh, goddess help us. It was one thing to trust Declan to guard the portal. Another entirely to leave him alone with my pregnant sister who was about to deliver the babies he'd been threatening to abscond with.

"I can stay," Axel said, but behind him, Bella was shaking her head.

"No, you go with Donna," she huffed. "Keep her safe for me."

"That goes double for you," I said to Declan. "Because I swear to all the stars in the heavens that if anything happens to my sister or her children, all anyone will find of you will be a greasy stain on the pavement."

The demon grinned at me. "Let's get her back to bed and you can work your magic."

"Bonnie, Clyde," I called when Declan and Bella had disappeared back into the manor. The gargoyles swooped in low and hovered in the air above me.

"Can the two of you protect the portal until we get there?" I asked.

"Oh yessum, little miss," Clyde said. "We can protect anything on the Storm Grove grounds, we surely can."

"Good." I would have to trust that the demon would take care of Bella and her babes. "Axel, go with them. I'll be there as soon as I can."

"No," Axel folded his arms over his chest, the picture of male stubbornness.

"What?" I blinked. That was the first time he'd ever said no to me.

"I can get you there faster." His eyes flickered with that purple lightning. "Trust me, Don."

I recalled how fast he could move, in the literal blink of an eye. "All right."

I nodded to the gargoyles who took wing before returning my attention to Axel. "Can you find Joseline and ask her to help Declan and Bella? Or better yet, run for the healer?"

"Do you think she'll come while we're under attack?" Axel asked.

"I don't know but I have to do everything I can to help Bella." Plus it would keep the werewolf girl away from whatever was about to happen. I didn't want Joseline in the middle of a battle.

"I'll find her, Don." He drew me to him once more, his nose buried in my hair.

"Are you all right?" I whispered.

"A little shaken up." He pulled back and looked down at me. "If Bella is right about what I am, I have more questions than answers."

I touched the golden stubble on his cheek. "We'll sort it all out."

If we got the chance.

Bella

"Aʜ!" I screamed as another spasm ripped through me. The pain had grown from a dull ache to an acute intense stab that stole my breath. "Oh goddess, I changed my mind. I don't want kids."

"Too late, witchling." The demon tried for his typical smirking tone but those flames still flickered in his eyes.

The demon I summoned was about to deliver my children. How had I gotten to this place?

Donna hurried into the room carrying sheets and towels. "There's water heating in the big cauldron on the stove," she said.

I reached for her hand and she took it. I didn't want her to leave. Not now, when I was enduring the biggest challenge of my life.

I looked at Declan. "Is guarding the portal really worth it?"

I didn't know what I wanted him to say. Keeping the blood off that portal had been my mission. If he said no, then I'd wasted my life. If he said yes, my sister would leave and perhaps even die in the effort to fight the wraiths.

"It must be done," Declan said. "It's your destiny."

"This is wrong," I gasped. "All wrong."

"Bella," Donna grabbed me by the shoulders and

held tight. "Look at me. You can do this. You are the strongest person I know."

I shook my head. How could she say that? I'd made so many mistakes. So many bad calls. "You're stronger."

She gripped my hand tight. "Nope, we are the same. One spark, two bodies. We've followed different paths, but they both led us to this moment. You've got this."

The pain eased and I gasped. "Okay. Okay."

"You researched this," Donna said.

It wasn't a question. "Until I fell asleep on my keyboard."

"I did the same thing before Devon was born." Donna gave me an easy smile. "Okay, you handle this and I'll go kick some wraith butt. Deal?"

I nodded. "Do it now, before another contraction hits."

She backed up and then looked at Declan. "This won't hurt her or the babies, will it? No brain damage?"

I'd forgotten about that part.

"Not if she's willing," the demon said. "It won't damage her any more than childbirth."

And didn't that make me feel just ducky?

Donna closed her eyes and when they opened they were pitch black. She began the chant to siphon. My own magic rose within me, heeding her call. And before I realized it I was looking at Declan.

I'd used my reflection on the demon before. And I'd seen nothing but the black fog that surrounded him. The dark power that marked him as what he was, a demon. But this time I saw something else. Like the sun breaking through a thick layer of storm clouds. The desire for one thing above all others. I saw the demon's soul.

And it was glorious.

"You," I began, not sure what I was going to say to him. It didn't matter. A wrenching from within. Not the babes. No, the tearing feeling was deeper. Soul deep. It was as though my entire body had been glued to a giant band-aid and was being ripped free.

The demon caught me as I fell back. His hands were so warm where he touched my cold skin. So cold. I looked back at him and saw only Declan.

Knowledge passed between the two of us. He had let me see that little bit of him. He trusted me not to betray him.

I felt humbled. And then pain as another contraction pulled all my focus down to my body.

"Is she all right?" Donna asked though her voice already sounded very far away.

"She'll be fine," Declan said as he scooped me up. "Let's get you in bed, witchling." His head swiveled to Donna as he scooped me up.

My sister moved forward and planted a kiss on my forehead, the same way our mother had done every night when we were children. "You got this. Believe me, Bells, this is the one that will stick."

Declan flicked his hand at her. "You have what you need. Go defend that portal."

Donna gave me one last look, her eyes changing from black to mirrored silver and back again. "I will."

And then she was gone.

The demon watched me for a minute as I huffed out a steady stream of air. Goddess preserve me, it hurt.

He smoothed my hair away from my face. "They are coming closer together."

"I can't give you what you want," I huffed.

"We'll see about that." A paper appeared in his hand. "Sign on the dotted line, witchling. I'd like to have this all settled before your children are born."

It was an effort to remember the Lamaze breathing and have a conversation at the same time. "Did anyone ever tell you you've got shit timing?"

He grinned and handed me the knife. "I wasn't the one foolish enough to summon a demon, now was I? Just an x will do. Then we can move on to more pressing matters."

"I'm not signing something I haven't read," I snapped.

Declan stared at me. "You can't be serious."

"Dead serious. Where's the rest of the contract?" I bitched at him. It felt good to get some of this aggravation out and the goddess knew he deserved it.

He shook his head. "Just when I think I've got you all figured out." The rest of the contract appeared and he handed it over.

Reading through all the fine points would be a decent distraction.

I needed one.

Donna

THE RAIN STARTED as Axel and I met in the foyer. Just a light sprinkle that made wet dots on the pavement. I could see the tops of the trees blowing sideways through the open front door. It was going to be a hell of a storm.

"Ready?" He offered me a hand and I was surprised to see that it shook a little. Was he nervous about the battle?

"Yeah." I curled my fingers through his.

"Whatever you do, don't let go." He turned and took a step.

And then time...slowed.

"What?" My mouth fell open. The raindrops seemed to hesitate in midair, as though they hadn't fully committed to falling. I glanced around, trying to take it all in.

That was when I saw Axel.

He was no longer the beautiful young man I'd known. His skin was gray, a darker color than the gargoyles. It felt leathery where we touched. Curved talons tipped the fingers that were still wrapped around mine. His veins were exposed, a pulsing purple that seemed to hum with energy. And he had wings. Not soft and feathery like a bird. They were membranous like a bat. They too thrummed with the same lightning veins I could see in his gray eyes. The wings jutted from the same places the scars had been when I'd seen them before.

I stared at him, trying to absorb it all. He was hideous. And glorious. Wickedly terrifying.

"I don't move fast," Axel cleared his throat. "Though I

guess it looks that way to everyone on the outside. I slow the world down."

Gods. The furies were born from gods. And not just any gods. Titans. I looked at him and felt Bella's power surge forward. I knew Axel was reflected in my gaze when he looked at me. Saw him swallow as he waited for my understanding.

For my judgment.

The thing Axel desired most was to be accepted. He feared my fear. Hated that he looked the way he did. His easy confidence was just a front for what lurked beneath the surface. A force of nature. It was a lonely mountain peak where he lived.

But the winds had shifted. I'd arrived with a heart full of hurt and an broken spirit that struggled and overcame because life had given me no choice. I'd made him want more. To be better. To live in his truth. Axel feared that now that he'd shown me the reality, I would pull away from him. And that action would confirm that he was just as monstrous as he'd always believed. Forever an outsider, never to find a true home.

"You're beautiful," I told him and leaned up on my tiptoes to kiss him lightly on the lips. "All of you. I'm glad you're on our side."

When I tried to pull away I felt his grip tighten as he clung to me with desperate strength.

"It makes me feel silly, that I was so worried about you before," I muttered.

His throat bobbed. "Don't. I've never had anyone care that much about me. I need you too, Don."

We walked between the raindrops, through the still

trees that were bent at odd angles, and against a wind that was held frozen. We moved slowly, steadily toward the portal.

"Look!" I pointed when I spotted Bonnie and Clyde hovering in midair, stone statues seeming to defy the law of gravity even as a crack of lightning illuminated them from behind.

He turned to face me. "When they see what I can do, the wraiths will swamp me. I've never faced an army before. I won't be able to hold time indefinitely. I can't protect you."

I squeezed his hand lightly. "You know one of the great things about thinking I was a defective dud all these years? It taught me how to take care of myself."

He smiled and stole one more kiss. "Ready to reenter time?"

"As I'll ever be."

Together we stepped forward into the world and whatever awaited us.

The first thing I did was summon air to create a shield around the portal. The same kind that had created Lewis's prison. I leaned my full weight against it. It wouldn't hold forever but as defenses went, it might buy us the time we needed.

The werewolves came first. Slinking through the trees on four paws, hackles raised. They fanned out, guarding the portal from the opposite side. I wanted to tell them to go, to run. These women had been through too much already and this wasn't their fight.

I met Kendra's eyes. She was easy to spot, the large gray and white wolf stood head and shoulders above the others. We stared at each other for a long moment. She bobbed her head once to me and I mouthed, "Thank you."

I hoped the wolves survived this. I hoped we all did. The wind howled and buckets of rain dumped down over our heads, soaking us through to the skin.

I wish I knew exactly how it was that Bella and I had combined our powers because I didn't relish the idea of killing people. Siphoning wasn't an exact science and doing a chant seven times in a row took time. I was going to have to rely on Axel and the wolves to keep the mob off me long enough to get through the spell.

"Someone's coming," Axel called against the driving rain. "Look at the wolves."

Fangs were bared, ears flattened. Weight shifted forward as though they were a heartbeat away from charging. I had no idea if they were waiting for a signal but then lost my train of thought as the first body emerged from the trees. One that moved with an easy grace that told me this person clearly wasn't wraith-ridden.

"You?" I asked, stunned.

"Surprise," the demon smirked.

CHAPTER 21
DONNA

I stared stupidly at Mindy, unable to wrap my wonky brain around the flames that flickered in her eyes. "You're the demon?"

"You're not much of a witch, Donna Sanders-Allen," Lewis's girlfriend said. "A demon steals your husband and you don't even realize what's happening?"

"You can keep Lewis," I told her. "Seriously. Take my husband, please. Ride him off into the sunset. Live happily ever after together. Just don't mix his whites with the colored clothes unless you want to listen to him bitch for a week straight."

She waved that away. "Lewis was a means to an end. And not a very effective end. I was hoping you and your sister would leave the portal unprotected as you came to deal with your divorce so my wraith-ridden could open it. But those damned wolves...." She sneered at Kendra."

Bella had been right all along, in her insistence that we protect the portal. The rain had plastered my hair to my face and I was tired of talking. "What the hell do you want?"

Those flames burned brighter. "The same thing you want, witch. To go home."

Slowly, I shook my head. "I can't let you open this portal,"

She shrugged her delicate shoulders. "Then I guess we're at an impasse. That's all right. I don't mind killing all of you. Your blood can be the sacrifice to open the gate."

Branches cracked loud enough to be heard over the rain. From ahead, from behind, the left, the right.

My heart thudded as a flash of lightning illuminated the dozens of dark shapes surging forward through the trees.

Mindy's smile grew as a blank-faced Lewis came up beside her. "Comeuppance won't save you, Donna Sanders-Allen. Not against one like me."

As one, the wraith-ridden humans rushed out from the trees.

Bonnie and Clyde swooped down. They each grabbed a person from the ground and used the body to knock dozens of others back, breaking the rushing line. Wolves charged forward, going for the throats. Axle moved at his enhanced speed, cutting a swath toward Mindy.

I focused on Lewis.

Yeah, he was a stain and he'd hurt me. He was still the father of my son. Comeuppance was a scorching case of herpes. Or maybe an audit from the IRS, not to be the blood sacrifice to open a demon portal. I focused on him and chanted.

. . .

Wind from the North
Wild and free
Siphon his power
So mote it be.

NOTHING HAPPENED. No scream or flinch. No sense of connection at all. Not like I'd felt with Annabeth or Nelson. I said the chant again, trying to focus Bella's magic as well as my own. The hoard didn't slow. Lewis smiled at me and I could see the wraith inside him.

What the shit? Why wasn't it working?

Because Lewis didn't *have* magic. The only power he'd ever had was over me because I gave it to him. He was a wraith-ridden mortal. They all were. Annabeth had been her own being.

We were so screwed.

Bella

"STRIKE THAT OUT," I huffed, curling around my midsection like a pill bug. "I'm not going to let you pay my credit card debt."

"Witchling," Declan growled and ran his hand through his disheveled hair. "The negotiations are over. You're about to give birth. Do you really want to quibble

243

over a few thousand dollars that I can summon out of the ether?"

"Yes!" I screamed as the wave of pain crested and broke. Tears were blurring my vision and the papers were damp from my sweating palms. "Goddess damn you, Declan. I am not a kept woman. I will not take your money. Not now. Not ever. Fuck. Directly. Off."

The last came out through my tightly gritted teeth.

He opened his mouth, most likely to argue with me, but was interrupted by the sound of shattering glass.

My head whipped around just in time to see the dark shape from my nightmares highlighted by the broken window.

"Hello, darling." Zeke Bradbury smirked at me from behind his magical shield.

I glared at the demon. This was lower than a snake's belly, bringing Zeke here, but Declan's brows were pulled together as he stared at the warlock. "How did you escape my containment spell?"

Zeke raised a brow "Who do you think summoned the other demon?"

Declan's lip curled up in a snarl. "Bella, sign the damn contract and let me kill this filth."

I glanced around but couldn't find the athame. Another contraction barreled down, hitting me with the impact of a freight train. Declan reached for the shield that surrounded Zeke. At the contact, it let off a hiss and a crackle of energy.

"Looks like I'm just in time," Zeke murmured as my stomach shifted. Wetness seeped between my thighs. "It won't be long now."

"Get out of here," I gasped. "These babies are mine."

"Not if you're dead," he shrugged. "Sanders legacy witches combined with Bradbury blood. If I can't siphon your magic this is the next best thing."

Declan prowled restlessly around the outside of the bubble. He had the strength to kill Zeke, especially without the other demon present, but he couldn't. Not unless I signed the contract in blood. And to do that I needed the damn knife.

Where was it?

I spotted the glint beneath the fold of the quilt at the same time Zeke did. He lunged for it but had to drop his shield to pick it up. Declan sprang like a great cat, knocking him to the ground. I fumbled with the athame, grabbing it by the black hilt. There was a blast of power and Declan flew across the room. I spotted the red glow around Zeke's neck coming from an odd-looking amulet. Demon power.

Declan slumped to the floor, knocked unconscious.

Zeke turned to face me. "Give me the dagger, Bella."

"Never." It was a pathetic defense compared to a warlock in his full power enhanced by demon magic. It was all I had.

"Did you really think you were better than me, you stupid bitch?" Zeke asked with narrowed eyes. "The high and mighty Sanders clan. Look at you now, the last of your line."

One chance. I doubled over on myself, gasping. He lunged.

The knife flashed out. Athames were ceremonial knives typically used for casting protection circles. They weren't always sharp. A knife was still a knife though and wielded by a witch in a fury it was more than enough.

Zeke's eyes went wide. He stumbled back. His hands rose to clutch the dagger even as a real contraction seized my body.

"If I'm a stupid bitch what does that make you?" I gasped as it passed. "You never could tell when I was faking it."

He staggered back into the window casing. Blood trickled from the corner of his mouth. He slumped to the ground, going boneless.

I panted. Incredible pressure swamped me. Along with the urge to push. "Declan!"

The demon was out cold. Had the blast from the amulet killed him?

Fear coursed through me.

Was I about to give birth on my own?

Donna

"Come on wonky brain, think!" I hissed as the gargoyles and werewolves fell back under the constant siege. Snaps and snarls filled the air. Axel was nowhere in sight. Had he been overcome by the sheer numbers?

Numbers. The cogs turned. The gears ground. That was it. The wraiths belonged to the demon. If I got rid of the demon, would the wraiths go too?

But how...?

My gaze fell on the portal. I swallowed hard. Grand's lessons had been clear. Under no circumstances were we ever to open the portal. But I had nothing else. Could I stuff one demon in without letting anything else out?

"Clyde, Bonnie," I shouted. "Keep me covered!"

The gargoyles swooped down just as a blast of demonic power shot out of the side.

"Careful, luv!" Clyde shouted as Bonnie narrowly avoided the strike. "That one almost got—"

He didn't get the chance to finish as the next beam struck him center mass.

"No!" Bonnie shouted as his body broke apart. I saw her round on the demon, her eyes promising retribution.

"Here!" I shouted to her. "I need you here, Bonnie!"

She swooped low and for a second I was worried she was going to ignore me, but then she plucked two bodies up and tossed them like bowling pins, clearing a path between me and the demon.

"You want it open?" I shouted to Mindy as I dropped the shield and stepped behind the line I'd drawn until I stood atop the portal. "Over my dead body."

"I don't see a problem with that!" The demon hurled another bolt of power at me. I resurrected the shield just in time.

Wraith-ridden bodies slammed into the shield, crushing the werewolves that snapped and snarled, fighting to free themselves from the press of bodies.

And then a blast of witchfire from the south. I turned and spotted Matilda Longshanks and several other members of her coven standing on the hilltop. She gave me a thumbs-up sign and then ignited another flame.

Mindy bared her teeth at the witches and shot off a beam of power but then Axel was there behind her. I saw the purple forks of lightning clash with the red as he seized her, trying to drag her into his time slip. To him, having slowed time to a crawl, the battle must have felt as though it went on for centuries.

"Make a hole!" I shouted to Bonnie who bowled more of the wraith-ridden out of the way, clearing the path for Axel. I saw Mindy shift and change, her body growing larger, her three-knuckled fingers appearing with wicked-looking horns. Axel held them inches away from his face as the demon Mindy tried to ram him.

They struggled. Then Lewis made a grab for Axel. Axel pivoted and the demon broke a hand free and swiped. I gasped as I saw blood spray up in an arc.

Then a fork of lightning crashed down, casting them both in sharp relief. When it had faded the demon went limp.

The purple blur streaked toward me. Axel staggered forward, bloody rents in his black t-shirt. "I can't go near the portal." he gasped.

I checked the immediate area but the counterattack had pulled many of the wraith-ridden away from the portal. I lowered the shield then snagged the demon's limp body and dragged it carefully over the line. "S'okay, I'll take it from here."

"What are you....?" Axel trailed and I saw the moment realization struck. "No, Don! You'll be sucked in, too."

"Tell my sister I love her," I shouted at him, then turned my back, unable to meet his agonized gaze. "And my son."

"Don," he bellowed.

But I'd fished my keyring out from my pants pockets. The one with the bows so neatly painted so I didn't fumble with the wrong keys and feel like an idiot. The one with the corkscrew at the end to open my emergency bottle of wine. Things that had seemed so damn important a week ago that I now realized were luxuries. Using the point on the corkscrew I pricked my finger and then squeezed out a single drop over the portal.

The ground shook. Lightning lit up the night. I felt a reverberation running through the shield. I'd hold it as long as I could and hopefully, Matilda Longshanks or one of the others could reestablish the seal after I was gone.

This hadn't been the plan.

"Don!" Axel shouted.

I turned to look at him and a single tear slipped down my cheek. The seal crumbled inward and I fell headlong into darkness.

CHAPTER 22

BELLA

S omething's wrong.

My twin tingle activated a warning. Donna was in trouble. My molars ground together. *She's not the only one.*

"Help," I begged the silent room. The pain and the urge to push were too much. My limbs trembled. I was smeared with blood. I'd thought I'd been prepared for a home birth, that I was ready to have these babies and do my level best to be the mom and mentor they needed. To pass on the legacy to the next generation. But I couldn't do it alone. "Please, someone, help us."

I'd tried to do everything right. So had Donna. How had it gone so horribly wrong?

Another contraction and then what felt like razors slicing through my insides. No, no, no. I sobbed, my body shaking. And then...

"Bella," a voice crooned.

I blinked through my tear-filled eyes and saw her face. "Mom?"

She smiled at me. Her face was so peaceful, lit from within. "You can do this, sweetheart. You need to hold on to your sister. Help hold her on the brink of this world as you bring your babies into it."

"How?" I gasped. "I don't have a spell. There's no one."

Mom reached out a hand and I took it, half expecting my hand to pass through. Instead, it closed around a golden cord. The feel of it was warm and soothing. And on the other end....

"Donna," I gasped as I sensed her. She was falling through darkness.

I didn't think. Instead, I forced my will, my very soul, into the rope. It became the umbilical cord that had sustained us in our mother's womb. When all we had known was each other. Before the world had conspired to tear us apart.

The cord snaked down and wrapped around Donna, pausing her midfall.

"I've got you," I said to my sister.

Magic flowed back to me through the bond. My magic of reflection, returning to its place of origin like a homing pigeon. And I showed Donna everything I saw when I looked at her. The strength. The pride I felt when I looked at her. She had survived and thrived in a world that I didn't know and then come roaring into her power when so many others would have quit.

The pain became a constant drumbeat in the background of my struggle. I held on to my sister, held on to the hope. Saw the reflection of myself in her eyes and felt my pride double.

A groan sounded from the far side of the room.

"Declan," I gasped.

"Witchling," he surged up and over to me.

"My sister," I panted. "Get her. Please."

"What?" His gaze fell on my body. "But the babies—"

"Get her!" I screamed as the pain tore through me. "I can't hold on much longer."

The demon turned to smoke and vanished.

"Hold on, Donna," I whispered into the darkness. "Help's on the way."

Donna

MADNESS SURROUNDED ME. I fell and fell and fell through the black depths of the portal. I couldn't see Mindy. I couldn't see my hand in front of my face. Far below something waited. Many somethings. All of them were hungry.

I shut my eyes. Not that it made a difference. But in my mind's eye, I saw the heavy golden chain. Felt the warmth of it. The love that radiated from it.

My sister. My light in the darkness. I reached for the tether and tried to wrap myself in its warm glow. Below me, I felt something else make a grab for it.

Demon Mindy.

"No," I snarled and felt the magic pour through me. Comeuppance to the demon who'd twisted souls into wraiths and sent them out into the world. Mindy, who'd destroyed my world as well as so many others in a bid for power. The demon army gathered below. Waiting.

"No," I said again. And then drew strength from the chain, from my sister's love. I would not let them pass. There was too much in the world above that I loved. Too much that needed protecting.

And then I saw her face. The other who'd sacrificed herself to keep the portal closed.

"Mom," I whispered.

"You've got this baby." She said and smiled. "It's been in you all along. Give them what they deserve."

The ghostly image faded. And my power grew. From the pit of my soul, it expanded outward, past what my flesh could contain. It radiated from me like light from a star. I heard them shriek as witch fire exploded out from my body like a sun going nova. Screams of pain, hisses of fear. The scrabbling of claws on stone.

My magic began to fade. The end was near. Then I would crash into the stone that was smeared with demon blood, as my mother had.

Hands snagged me. Instead of crashing into stone, I was held against an unyielding body.

Lightning flashed around me as Axel held me. My gaze shifted up and I saw...,

Those wings. Wings made of pure energy, purple and blue jagged streaks that cut sharply through the relentless dark.

"Gotcha," He grinned at me and pulled me close. The gashes on his chest were cauterized. By his wings? "Never letting you go."

"How?" I croaked an instant before I saw the flames,

JENNIFER L. HART

and felt the encompassing mist that Declan used to travel.

"Retract your power, witch," the demon grunted. "I haven't been as evil as some, but this still stings like a bitch."

I sucked in air and pulled my power back inside my skin.

The fog sighed as though relieved and then we were rising up and up and up out of the portal.

The demon faded away and Axel flapped his wings, carrying us back away from the portal. I was entranced by the jumping pulses of energy.

Bodies lay everywhere. Wolves and humans too. "Are they dead?"

"No," Axel said. "They went unconscious when you fell. There was this noise as all the wraiths were destroyed. Dozens of shrieks at once. It must have over-loaded the wolves' hearing."

"It worked then." I sagged against him. "We did it."

I spotted the witches picking their way through the throng. Bonnie kneeling beside a pile of rubble.

Axel didn't stop though. "You did it, Don."

"But?" I asked as I looked over my shoulder at the giant gaping hole that had been a sealed portal.

"That can wait. Your sister needs you." He held me close and the world around us froze, the smoke and embers held immobile in midair.

We beat the demon back to the house. Axel didn't bother with the door, just flew in through the smashed window where Bella lay unconscious on the bed.

254

I shoved out of his hold the second his feet hit the floor, distantly registering the corpse in the corner.

"Get the healer," I shouted at Axel as I rushed to Bella's side. "Now."

Her eyes opened at the sound of my voice. She was deathly pale, her lips dried and cracked. "Donna?"

I ran for her, ignoring the soot and blood that streaked my hands. "I'm here, Bells. You saved me."

She looked utterly exhausted. I worried that even the healing would be too much for her.

"I saw Mom," she rasped. "She was here. She helped me save you."

My eyes watered. "I know. I saw her too."

"You have to take care of them," Bella whispered. "The twins. Teach them how to be strong, like you."

I shook my head. "You'll teach them yourself."

"Tired," she whispered and her lids fluttered closed.

"If I may," the demon said from behind me. "You need to give her strength."

I shot him a look over my shoulder. "You mean siphon my power into her? I'm almost tapped out."

"Not yours." His eyes glowed. "Mine."

Bella

THE PLACE I'd reached was do or die. I would either make it through to the other side of this battle...or I wouldn't.

My sister had come back. I could hear her voice, brisk and sharp, the way it always sounded when she was worried. Was she arguing with someone? I was glad it wasn't me.

I'd saved her and now she had come to save my children. She was a good mom. She would do right by them.

Then I felt a touch. Calloused hands on my cheek, the fingers too long and palms too broad to be Donna's. "An X on the line, you stubborn little witchling."

"What?" My brows creased and I felt the sharp pinch as something pricked my finger. "Ouch."

"Stubborn is right," Donna bitched as she drew my bleeding hand to a tattered piece of paper. "When a man wants to pay off your credit cards no questions asked, you let him."

The x was wobbly but there was a flash and then the paper flamed up, leaving nothing but the acrid tang of smoke behind.

And then Donna began chanting.

"What are you doing?"

And the rush of power washed through me. Unlike the cool waves from Annabeth or Nelson, this was hot, like tongues of fire.

Demonic fire.

It zipped through my system, turning my blood to lava. Raw power coursed through me, unlike any magic I'd ever known.

"I'll take the kiss you owe me now, summoner," Declan said.

The demon had the worst timing. My lips parted and I prepared to tell him so but then his sealed over mine.

Hot, blazingly hot. It lifted me out of the pain, almost out of my body.

And then it was gone, leaving me thrumming with demonic heat.

"Stand aside," a no-nonsense voice with a familiar Yankee accent demanded. "There are some babies that need to be born. And for the love of the goddess, would someone get that dead man out of here?"

I looked up at Declan who seemed paler than usual. No fire because he had lent me his strength.

"You still owe me a date, witchling," he murmured.

"Mind if she gives birth first?" Matilda Longshanks quipped.

The next several minutes were a flurry of activity. Donna scooted onto the bed behind me smelling of smoke and blood. Axel and Declan dragged Zeke's corpse away. And I panted and pushed, hoping it wasn't too late for my babes.

"One big push!" the healer ordered.

I grunted and did as she commanded, juiced with demon magic and determination.

"I can see a head!" Matilda announced. "With the next contraction. One more big push and we'll get the shoulders."

My body did the impossible. Bones rearranged, muscles clenched, and then...

"It's a girl," Matilda grinned up at me and a moment later a cry filled the room.

"Shocker," Donna nudged me as Matilda cleaned my daughter up. "Name?"

I shook my head. "What does she look like?"

"A pissed-off craisin," my sister said as Matilda put the baby in my arms.

"Astrid," I breathed as I looked at my daughter. And then. "Oh goddess, I think the other one is coming."

Donna took the baby and I braced as the griping pains resumed.

"This one's stuck," Matilda's spider brows drew together.

"Thanks for telling me that." I gritted. "I never would have figured that out on my own."

Time seemed to slow and narrow down to that single point of concentration. I huffed and puffed and then finally, the second baby came into the world.

"What is it?" I asked after a moment when no one spoke. Donna was jiggling the first baby back and forth. "Is she all right?"

Matilda had her hands over the baby, her white healing light working. "He will be. The cord was around his neck, but we got to him in time."

"Him?" Donna and I said in unison.

"See for yourself," the healer held out the naked baby.

Sure enough, a little penis was clearly visible.

"Huh," Donna said. "I guess we really are more alike than we ever thought."

My son, *my son*, started to wail. The healer cleaned him and then gave him to me.

"See, it's a good thing I didn't think of two girls' names," I rasped. "This one is going to be Ember."

"Stars and fire." Donna nodded. "Perfect. Welcome to the family."

CHAPTER 23
DONNA
TWO WEEKS LATER....

I had the dream again. The huge house that I had to get in order. The stuff that was everywhere. Strangers who shoved their way into the space that was perfect for me.

This time though, it didn't overwhelm me. This time I knew.

The strangers had come to help. Would help, if I let them in.

I opened my eyes and stared out at the morning light. I knew where I had to go.

The walk through the forest helped me stretch my stiff muscles. I'd finished Ali Smith's job the day before. Fifty Shades of Geritol had been replaced by a space up to code and ready for a tenant. Ali had been thrilled with the result and I'd decided to take a few weeks off, to handle some personal business.

When I reached the clearing I paused and looked at the scorched earth surrounding the sinkhole. I'd come here every day, hoping I could detect any hint of my mother's presence.

"I miss you," I said to her. "I'm sorry I didn't believe."

A soft breeze caressed my cheek, like a gentle touch. Full of understanding. And forgiveness.

"That's a big hole."

"I bet you say that to all the girls." I didn't bother to turn away from the cauterized portal to face him. "What are you doing here, Lewis?"

Twigs snapped as he shifted from side to side. "I, uh, wanted to apologize. For the things I said. I don't remember much after the other day."

He wouldn't. The wraith-ridden people who'd been freed when Mindy and I fell had no memory of what had happened or how they'd come to Storm Grove. We'd done tactful interviews as we arranged for their transportation home. Many were locals, but several were from Florida.

"Did you ever go to Florida with Mindy?" I asked Lewis.

He jumped as though I'd stuck a live wire in his ear. "Yeah. Jacksonville. For a conference last month. Why does it matter?"

"Just curious." According to Bella, Lewis hadn't been wraith-ridden when he'd been screwing around with Mindy. I didn't think he'd been compelled, either. Just weak and skeevy.

He cleared his throat. "So yeah, that whole thing with Mindy? It was a mistake. And I was wondering if maybe...." He trailed off.

I turned my attention away from the defunct portal and looked at him.

"You wanted to come home?" His voice went up on the last word as though he held out hope.

I didn't say a word. I watched him. The sad, powerless man I'd tried so hard to please. He'd made me feel special, once. When I'd given him a son. Before the little digs had started. Insults about the family I'd come from or how I didn't finish what I started.

What was the comeuppance for my husband? Had he learned anything? I had, both about my marriage and myself. So what if he hadn't cherished me or the joy I'd brought into his life? That didn't mean there hadn't been joy. Neither of us could get those years back. But we could move forward.

"No, Lewis. It's over. File the papers, sell the house."

He blinked. "Seriously? You're going to stay here?" He looked around the clearing, not seeing what I saw.

Footsteps sounded behind me. I felt his electric presence a moment before an arm draped across my shoulders. "Yeah, she is." Axel drawled.

If his eyes had gotten any wider Lewis's eyeballs would have popped out of his skull. I raised a brow. Would he comment on the age difference? Did I even care?

But, ever the chickenshit, Lewis didn't say what he was thinking. He'd scurry away, maybe call his blowhard brother and complain about how I was the one having a midlife crisis. Maybe Devon too. That thought hurt my heart. I'd contact my son later and explain everything.

Leaving out the business with the demons, and of course, the fury I was falling for.

"Want me to escort him out, babe?" Axel asked and pressed a kiss to my hand.

I shook my head. "Nah. He knows his way. Goodbye, Lewis. Watch out for the thorns along the path. I'd hate to see you get caught."

We managed to keep straight faces all the way into the woods. I cracked first and pressed my back into the trunk of a live oak. "Oh goddess, did you see his face?"

"Were you tempted to go back to him?" Axel's eyes flashed with lightning and the ghost of his wings wrapped around me.

I pretended to think about it. "Well, all my clothes are there and my favorite wineglasses...,"

I cut off with a shriek as Axel tickled me. "Stop, stop," I squealed, trying to catch my breath.

He pressed his forehead into mine. "So, no regrets then?"

I tried to push him away, but couldn't. My fingers ended up gripping his gray t-shirt, holding him close. He smelled of ozone and spring rain. "I keep telling you this isn't a good idea," I whispered.

"We'll have to agree to disagree," he murmured. His lips brushed over mine in a light kiss.

A low growl came from our right and we broke away from each other. Joseline stood there in wolf form. She gave us a tail tip wag.

I let out a slow breath. "Naptime must be over. I promised Bella we'd watch the twins this afternoon."

He raised an eyebrow. "Chaperones is it? You can't avoid me forever, Don."

I winked at him. "I can do anything I set my mind to."

Bella

"Ice cream?" I asked the demon at my side. "That's your idea of a first date?"

Declan wore sunglasses, hiding any tell-tale flickers from view. "They have fifty-four flavors and so far I've only sampled thirteen. If you get one and give me a taste that's two more."

"I feel so used." I shook my head and stepped up to the counter. "One chocolate peanut butter cup, please, and one...." I raised a brow at Declan.

"Mint chocolate chip," he decided.

I made a face. "You know those two really don't go together. Chocolate and peanut butter, yes. Chocolate and mint, yes. Mint and peanut butter, not so much."

"I probably shouldn't try and take food from a nursing mother, anyhow." He took out his wallet and flashed me a smirk.

"I can pay for myself," I fumbled for my purse but he gripped my hand.

"No, witchling. I'm paying for the pleasure of your company. This was my idea so I'm footing the bill."

The touch unnerved me. It was as close as we had

come to one another since that kiss. I huffed out a sigh and moved away to sit at a table in the shade. We were in the death throes of summer and the dry grass crackled underfoot. It hadn't rained since the night the twins were born. I was trying not to read into it, but legacy witches were highly attuned to the change of seasons. Maybe I could talk Donna into doing a cleansing and revitalizing ritual.

"Penny for your thoughts," Declan murmured as he handed me my ice cream cone. Which had a big bite taken out of it.

I glared up at him and then sighed. "You'd get change back."

"Thinking about the fury?" He asked and took a lick of his mint chocolate chip, making the innocent act seem almost lewd.

I'd been trying not to think about what my assistant was. If I'd found out before Donna had come back to Storm Grove, I might have fired him but my sister had grown so attached. "Is there any way to help him?"

"He is what he is, witchling." Declan shrugged. "You can't change him."

"Yes, but you are what you are and you're not all bad." He'd siphoned his strength to me to get through giving birth to my son and daughter. No, the demon wasn't all bad. I still didn't want to be in his debt.

Ice cream was starting to drip down my arm and I took a hasty lick. Then made a moaning sort of sound and closed my eyes. "Oh, that's so good it's positively sinful."

It took me a moment to realize the demon had gone

totally still. It took another moment to realize what he was reacting to. Namely, my ice cream-induced orgasm.

He smiled at me. "You know something? I'd wager that under the right circumstances, different flavors might pair perfectly."

My teeth sank into my lower lip. "Maybe you're right."

Neither of us was talking about ice cream.

***

Donna

"AND WHO'S the cutest little fat baby?" I cooed to my nephew in that voice reserved for talking to babies, animals, and idiots. "You are. Yes, you are!"

"You're gonna give him a complex, Don." Axel shook his head as he rocked Astrid on his left side. Her eyelids were starting to droop.

"I can't help it," I said as I leaned over the blanket. "He's such a little beefcake. Aren't you, Ember? Aren't you a tasty little beefcake? Oh! I just want to eat you right up!"

I made gobbling sounds and blew a raspberry on his belly button and he gurgled merrily.

"See, this is how witches get bad raps," my sister said as she breezed through the door.

I raised a brow at her. "What, no demon entourage?"

"He had to head out of town. He's bought another place out on the coast and wants to check on the progress." She smiled and flushed. "We went out for ice cream."

"Be still my heart." I winked at her and noted her flushed cheeks. "I take it everything went well?"

"Don't." Bella held up a hand.

"Don't what?" I feigned innocence.

"Nothing is going to happen. I'm just fulfilling the contract." Bella moved to where Axel stood to take her daughter. "To the letter. I don't want to be in his debt."

Like we could ever repay him. I was convinced the demon had helped save both of our lives, though when I'd asked, he'd said he was just being a team player. Right. Eventually, I would figure out what comeuppance looked like for him.

"I'm heading into town to grab some stuff for dinner," Axel said. "Any requests?"

I shook my head though I smiled up at him. "I trust you."

He bent down and kissed me on the forehead. "Be back soon, gorgeous."

Oh man, I was going to cave in like a sinkhole. How could I not?

Bella set the sleeping Astrid in her basket, but I didn't miss the concerned look on her face.

"What?" I asked.

"You know what he is," she hissed. "If he flips out I don't want you to be collateral damage."

I scooped Ember up and brought him to my sister so she could nurse. Even though Ember had been smaller than his sister at birth, his lusty appetite had helped him pack on the pounds with gusto.

"I know who he is," I said. "And what he's done. I think that's a hell of a lot more important than some story in the grimoire. "

With Ember settled against her breast, she reached out her other hand to me. "I just got you back so forgive me if I'm being paranoid. I want you to be happy, Donna."

"Back at you." I squeezed her hand and then jumped as the doorbell rang.

We stared at each other. "Are you expecting someone?" I asked.

She shook her head. "You?"

"No." I hurried to get it before the gong sounded again and woke Astrid.

The doors swung inward and the first thing I saw was an older woman with bright pink hair fussing over the vacant spot where Clyde had once sat. Axel was trying to glue him back together, but he hadn't found all the pieces yet.

"Can I help you?" I asked her. She blinked at me through lenses as thick as coke bottles and then turned to address someone I couldn't see. "Is that her?"

"Yes," said a familiar voice. I turned and spied the diminutive form of Ali Smith as she made her way up the steps.

"Ali." I blinked, surprised. "What are you doing here? Is everything all right with the room?"

"Oh yes, dear. Don't worry. My sister and I are here on an entirely different errand."

"Your sister?" I blinked. The two women looked nothing alike. Tippy could've wrestled alligators in her youth, whereas Ali appeared fragile as if a stiff wind would knock her over. Of course, not all siblings were like me and Bella. Remembering my manners, I stood back and gestured inside. "It's nice to meet you. Won't you come in?"

"Tippy White," The pink-haired woman stuck out her hand and shook with all the vim and vigor of a lumberjack half her age. *Mental note, don't ask Tippy to arm wrestle.*

They shuffled in. I gestured toward the sitting room. Too bad Axel was gone. I was sure he would have whipped up the perfect tray of refreshments for them. But I could handle basic cocktails. "Can I get you something to drink? We have a pitcher of lemon and hibiscus sun tea."

"Anything stronger?" Tippy asked.

I eyed the bar. "Gin and tonic? Rum and coke?"

"One of each." Tippy nodded firmly.

"The tea sounds lovely," Ali added.

Bemused, I fixed the drinks and after pouring an iced tea for myself sat across from the sisters. "So, what is it I can help you with?"

"We need you to help us find someone," Tippy declared and knocked back her first drink.

My lips parted. "Um, I'm not sure that I'm the right person for that," I said slowly. "Have you tried the police? Or maybe a private investigator?"

"It's not that kind of search, dear." Ali clarified. "We detected something a few weeks ago. Something we haven't felt in years. And it came from this property."

"What—?" I began and then trailed off as both

women looked at me. Two sets of eyes forked with purple lightning.

I got up and went to the bar. I needed something stronger, too.

A quick note from the author

HELLO AND THANK you for reading *Midlife Magic Mirror*! I hope you have enjoyed meeting Donna and Bella Sanders. And yes, if you put their names together you get "Belladonna" a natural poison. So totally intentional in case you were wondering!

I've always been fascinated with the idea of comeuppance—you know when the evildoer gets what's coming to them. But not everyone is a good guy or a demon. And as we see there is a bit of wiggle room even with the demons in this world. So in giving Donna the "dud" the power of comeuppance, I've essentially created a character who is required to meet justice. Plus how many of us would like to contain our ex's in an invisible box for a few hours?

A few housekeeping notes. This book was originally published in serial format on Kindle Vella in May of 2023 under the title *Legacy Witches of Shadow Cove* and my pen name, Gwen Rivers. A few changes include Ethan becoming Declan. I already have an Ethan character in the Silver Sisters series and try not to repeat character names. As we all know, names hold power! The other change was the added scene suggested by my proofreader, who wanted to see Donna and Bella hash out the whole did Bella ever sleep with Axel question. Mental forehead smack on that! Of course we needed some closure there!

So what's next? Wondering what it would be like to make a bet with a demon? Keep reading to see Bella do just that in Midlife Magic Monster, book 2 in the Legacy Witches series. And sign up for my author newsletter for behind-the-scenes info on what's cooking in the Word Witch's cauldron.

Love and light,

Jennifer L Hart.

Midlife Magic Monster

"You've been staring into that water for almost an hour now, witchling," the demon crooned from behind me. "If the images aren't coming to you, you should probably—"

"What? Give up?" I snapped.

Declan, the name the demon had chosen while in his mortal guise, raised one dark eyebrow. "It's not a criticism of your abilities. There are many forces in this world. Stronger and more horrifying than even your darkest imaginings. There is absolutely nothing more tragic than a witch who doesn't know her limits."

I shoved my hair out of my face. "You don't get it. I can feel it in my bones. A storm is coming. We weren't prepared for the last one. We need to be ready for whatever comes next."

Declan crouched down beside me and peered into the water. "Divination doesn't just show us what's coming. It shows us answers to the questions we're too afraid to ask. You know this storm is brewing under your own roof. Maybe you need to admit that to yourself before asking the universe for more."

I blew out a sigh and leaned back in the chair, closing my eyes. They burned from so much intent focus. "You're talking about Axel."

"Even demon kind doesn't fuck with the furies. Yet you and your sister are hiding one from the other two?" He made a *tsking* sound. "That won't end well, witchling."

"It's not my choice." I hadn't known what Axel was when I'd first offered to take him on as my assistant. He'd been there when I'd needed someone, and I'd had a feeling I should keep him close.

"You're keeping a viper in your garden." Declan picked an invisible piece of lint off his power suit. The scruffy stubble that coated his strong chin matched the jet black hair and eyes. He was the epitome of a high-powered hotel mogul. No one would ever suspect that the exterior was a glamor which hid a centuries-old creature. "Have you tried the banishing spell we discussed?"

I nodded. "I started it on the last full moon. So far, nothing."

The spell was intended to make an unwanted person disappear from your home. As the moon waned to darkness, the urge to disappear became more and more overwhelming. Every evening when the moon rose, I'd written Axel's name on a piece of paper each night and burned it in a black candle that I'd coated with red pepper flake and poppy seeds to cause irritation and confusion. "Maybe I need a stronger irritant. A Carolina Reaper."

"What you need is patience," the demon crooned. "You really must stop playing with fire, witchling. One of these days you'll burn the entire town to the ground."

The sexy demon was too close and smelled far too tempting. Everything about him called to me. The expensive clothes, the feral dark looks all dark spice and provocative heat.

The tingling feelings made me snappish. "What would you have me do?"

He tugged at the snowy white cuff of his dress shirt. "What I advised you to do when you first realized furies were living in town. Turn him over to them."

"Donna's infatuated with Axel." I shook my head back and forth. "I can't do that to her."

Though I would never say it to Declan, I feared Donna would break if she were forcibly separated from Axel. Though my sister would never admit it, she was a clinger. She clung to me in the early years. Before my magic had manifested and hers hadn't. Then she clung to her pantload of a husband until Devon was born. She'd been living for that kid for the last eighteen years. Having him head off to college to live his own life was a challenge for her. Adding magic and divorce to the mix had upended her neat little applecart. She'd latched onto Axel the way a drowning woman would latch on to a life preserver. I couldn't fire him and rip away the only thing that was keeping her afloat.

"So, what's your plan?" Declan rose from the three-legged stool in front of his magical workbench and offered me a hand.

I ignored it. Having the demon touch me was...unsettling. Instead, I got to my feet and headed for the door. Odd how I'd grown used to the sulfur smell of the demon's inner sanctum. Declan himself had almost shed the scent but the enclosed places where he'd first worked magic when he'd arrived in our world still contained the distinctive demon odor.

"The plan is to reconnect with my sister. Once she realizes that she has me and the twins, she won't feel as dependent on Axel."

Declan snorted. "Do you really think it's so simple?"

My shoulders had grown stiff from being hunched over the scrying bowl for so long. "Why wouldn't it be? Men are expendable. Sisters are forever."

"Would you care to make a wager on that?" The demon smirked.

I shook my head. "No way. I'm not betting on my sister's relationship."

"Why not? If you're so confident that this is, how did you phrase it? A fling? Why not take an unlosable bet."

I hesitated. "Why should I?"

"Because if you win, I'll teach you any spell you wish." He waved at the wall that held ancient scrolls and dusty tomes, the wealth of knowledge demon kind had collected over the eons.

My gaze roved over the forbidden knowledge. Curiosity gnawed at me. Demon magic was strictly forbidden to witches. It was one of the first lessons Grand had drilled into us as kids. I could still see her straight-backed countenance as she lectured us.

"No matter how great your need, you must never give in to the temptation to use demon magic."

"Why?" I'd asked. "Legacies don't believe in dark and light. Magic is magic."

Grand had dipped her head in a regal nod. "True, but that's witch magic. The demons were banished from this plane for interfering with choice. They created those abominable wraiths to take over a mortal's will. That sort of corruption spreads if you don't stamp it out. If you are ever tempted to practice demonic magic, the rest of your kind will toss you into the portal where you will be preyed upon by demons for the rest of your existence."

The severe warning had stuck with me. But I still had questions. What could demons do that we didn't even know about? So much had been lost during the burning times, when lines of legacy witches had been broken and family members turned on one another. Historically speaking our line was relatively new. So much had been lost. And thinking of my sister and children with a potentially mad fury in proximity made me wonder what sort of protection spells Declan's magic vault contained.

"Fine," I agreed. What could it hurt? Other than nearness, Donna and Axel had very little in common. She had an itch and was using him to scratch it. I felt confident that given time, her infatuation would flame out and then I'd be free to terminate his employment or hand him over to the furies. "And what if I lose? Which I won't."

His lips curved up in a seductive smile. "If you lose, you'll agree to part with something very dear to you."

"No sex," I said, pointing right at him. "I won't whore myself for a bet."

"No sex," he agreed and extended his hand. "Is it a deal?"

I hesitated. Declan had agreed to no sex way too quickly. Did that mean he wasn't interested in me that way? And why did that thought...sting?

Not that I was looking for a lover. And never a demon.

But if not for sex, what did he want? What if...no. It was irrelevant. I wouldn't lose.

Clasping my hand in his I ignored the crackle of energy that sparked between us and spoke the binding words, "It's a bargain well struck."

Heat filled his dark gaze. "Oh, witchling. We're going to have so much *fun*."

Buy Midlife Magic Monster Now!

Made in the USA
Las Vegas, NV
19 July 2024

92566430R00157